A Great Escape

They came to an agreement. Though they didn't understand how it could happen, they decided that if they should ever find themselves in that strange outside world, each would make for the windmill. It was to be a gathering point, and there they would wait for one another.

By the same author:

The Ram of Sweetriver
The King of the Vagabonds
The Beach Dogs
Just Nuffin

The Farthing Wood Series:

Animals of Farthing Wood
In the Grip of Winter
Fox's Feud
Fox Cub Bold
The Siege of White Deer Park
In the Path of the Storm

A Great Escape

Colin Dann

RED FOX

For Andy

A Red Fox Book
Published by Random Century Children's Books
20 Vauxhall Bridge Road, London SW1V 2SA

A division of the Random Century Group

London Melbourne Sydney Auckland
Johannesburg and agencies throughout the world

First published by Hutchinson Children's Books 1990
Red Fox edition 1991
Reprinted 1991

Text © Colin Dann 1990

The right of Colin Dann to be identified as the author of this work has been asserted by him in accordance with the Copyright, Designs and Patents Act, 1988

Printed and bound in Great Britain by
Cox & Wyman Ltd, Reading, Berkshire

ISBN 0 09 977150 5

Contents

— 1 —

Inside the Shop

The man and the boy were arguing again. The bewildered animals listened to the noise. Ever since the boy had come to the shop to help there seemed to have been disharmony. It had become steadily worse. The animals were used to the old man. He had always tended them and they hadn't the knowledge or capacity to understand that he didn't tend them all that well. They were fed; now and then their cages were cleaned; occasionally the old man would pause long enough to talk to them or even give a brief caress. And that was all they knew about it until the boy had come along. He was quite different.

For a start he was much brisker and more certain in his movements. He spoke in a different way to the people who came into the shop and sometimes took one of the animals away with them. And he spoke to them – the animals – differently too. He spoke to them as often as he could and they enjoyed the sound of his voice. It made them feel relaxed and comfortable. But when he spoke to the old man they didn't feel relaxed and comfortable at all, because the old man didn't seem to like the boy very much, even though they were together all the time. The animals thought the boy sensed this and it was then that the arguing began. It made them tense and nervous. There was an argument going on now. The voices crackled and the noise zipped back and forth across the shop. But, oddly enough, it would cease instantly when another person came in from outside. The animals wished for somebody to appear now. Even old Auntie, who was the oldest incumbent of the Windmill Pet Shop and seemed to understand human speech (she could certainly make the same sort of noises), squawked edgily from her perch by the counter once or twice.

'I tell you to leave the cages, Eric!' the old man was shouting. 'They're clean enough. You're here to serve the customers!' He gave the lapels of his ancient shop coat an assertive yank.

'But there aren't any customers at the moment, Mr Dobson,' the boy replied. He was taller than the proprietor and he looked down at him with an irritating half-smile.

'Are you going to do as I tell you or not?' cried the old man. 'Because if not . . .' His grey eyes glinted. His face and bald pate flushed angrily.

The boy shrugged. He understood the implied threat. 'What shall I do, then, while I'm waiting?'

'Oh! Go and replenish the water bowls or something,' spluttered the old man, turning on his heel. He shuffled to the rear of the shop, pulling at his ragged moustache.

The boy scratched his spiky red hair and started to whistle half-heartedly. Then he saw the old man's steely eye on him and stopped. He began to go around the cages and boxes and glass tanks in order, removing the water bowls and refilling them. Some of the cages were vacant. These were the large ones reserved for puppies and kittens. The last of these had been sold some time ago and Joel Dobson didn't plan to replace them. His stock of animals had dwindled to a fraction of what had been customary in his shop in earlier days. He had allowed this to happen deliberately. He was sixty-eight years old. He had lost his enthusiasm for the shop and he was winding the business down. The premises needed decorating, the fitments were old-fashioned, the shop was generally grubby and Dobson himself was careless of his appearance. The entire place had a run-down look about it. This was what Dobson and the boy Eric usually argued about. Eric thought the shop owner was being unkind to his animals, keeping them in squalid surroundings.

Actually the old man was not intentionally unkind. He loved animals and his fondness for them had led him to invest in a pet shop in the first place. He and his wife had run the business quite happily for years. But when Mrs Dobson died suddenly the bereaved man had lost all zest for life, including the Windmill Pet Shop. He had let things slide and the only reason customers still came to his shop was because Eric was responsible for ordering and maintaining supplies of pet food and didn't permit the shop to run short of anything, from meat and dog biscuits to millet sprays for budgerigars and maggots for goldfish. Moreover, the Windmill Pet Shop was the only shop selling pet food in the small country town of Wandle. As far as pets themselves were concerned, however, Joel Dobson had made up his mind that, once all his livestock was sold, he would keep no more. When the last animal went he intended to close down. The only thing was, now that there was only a handful of animals remaining in the shop, he found he could hardly bear to part with them. It was as if he was trying to hold off the day when the Windmill Pet Shop, which he had run for twenty-five years, closed for ever. And that was why Eric argued about the plight of the residue of pets which comprised a hamster, a rat, a guinea pig, a rabbit, a tortoise, a monkey and old Auntie, the grey parrot.

After shop hours, when Eric went home, Auntie was allowed brief exercise flights around the shop. Then the old man would call her to her perch where he would re-fix her chain. Auntie was quite used to this routine and raised no objection. When Dobson retired to his living quarters above, the animals talked amongst themselves.

Their cages and containers were ranged along two sides of the shop, away from the front entrance. The counter was at the back. In the middle of the area were shelves of pet food for every requirement, together with birdcages, fish tanks, dog collars and leads, medicines and other paraphernalia. Since the premises were small, the animals were able to hear each other perfectly well even if they couldn't see everyone else. On the left-hand side there were several empty tanks once used to house goldfish, tropical fish and terrapins. Next to these, in a dry roomy aquarium, was Pebble the tortoise. He spent most of the day dozing in his bed of straw when he wasn't eating, but later he enjoyed taking part in the conversations. In fact he was usually the one to make the first comment. He would peer through the side of his glass box at his immediate neighbours, the rat Pie and Thrifty the hamster who occupied separate boxes.

'Trouble again today,' was, these days, almost invariably his opening remark.

Pie and Thrifty had become so used to hearing it they often didn't bother to respond at once. Sometimes one of the other animals – Skip the rabbit or Candyfloss the guinea pig who shared a cage on the other side – would answer sooner.

'We expect it now, don't we?' one of them would say. Or, 'It really can't go on like this.'

All of the animals expected the ructions between the man and the boy to reach a climax very soon which would result in one of them gaining the upper hand and dominating the other permanently. They understood nothing of human working relationships. The macaque monkey Spider, whose cage was the largest, widest and tallest of all, would swing with effortless acrobatics from rung to rung of his climbing frame as he listened to the humbler intellects of the pet shop's company. Then he would pause and deliver a pithy comment from his store of superior wisdom.

He was a small monkey about the size of a terrier. His hair was buff-coloured with a darker stripe along the back and a short of crest on the crown.

From the top of his cage he could see the entire shop interior. He could see, too, beyond the shop's glass frontage to the world beyond, where the land fell away from the hillside on which the building stood at the edge of the town, revealing woods, fields and houses and, most prominent of all, the windmill which gave the shop its name, at the top of a hillock. This windmill was a landmark for miles around. It could be seen by all the animals from some point in their restricted little homes and it was a focal point for them all. Spider was not officially for sale. He was being fostered by the old man as a favour to a friend, the animal's rightful owner, who had gone abroad for a lengthy spell. Dobson had received permission to sell the monkey should the right sort of customer show interest. Otherwise he was to remain where he was. And remain he had – for nine months.

From his position of vantage at the top of his cage, Spider could see the rows of empty cages and pens and boxes which had been fully occupied on his arrival. The vacant puppy and kitten pens were next to Skip and Candyfloss's cage. The monkey was able to assess the difference between the appearance of the shop now and as it had once been and he had formed an opinion. He was sure the old man would rid himself one by one of the small animals, leaving only him – Spider – and old Auntie behind. He dreaded this eventuality because Auntie wouldn't be much of a companion, sharp as she was. The other animals, despite their generally inferior intelligence (except for Pie – he was clever) were more companionable. The trouble with old Auntie was, she had been there too long. She was a fixture of the place, Joel Dobson's own pet, and she couldn't – or wouldn't – think about what was outside the confines of her immediate surroundings. The other animals had at one time been equally unimaginative. But, ever since the boy's arrival, their attitude had changed. They all sensed

6

that he offered them something beyond that which they had previously experienced – something additional to the monotony of their present existence. It was from his manner, his voice, his look that they derived their feeling. It was a sort of instinctive reaction. So they all hoped that Eric would emerge as the superior of the two humans when the crisis was reached.

Meanwhile, at Spider's instigation, they dreamed of the life that lay outside their little intimate world; what it would be like to sit below the great wide sails of the windmill that seemed to them so like arms flung out, beckoning to them. How different they would feel as they sat there, looking back at that little world of the shop and they tried to imagine what it would be like to make the journey from one to the other.

Then they came to an agreement. Though they didn't understand how it could happen, they decided that if they should ever find themselves in that strange outside world, each would make for the windmill. It was to be a gathering point, and there they would wait for one another.

—— 2 ——

The Door is Opened

Early morning was a good time to talk. The animals always awoke at daybreak before old Dobson was around. Candyfloss, the guinea pig, often wondered what had happened to her old companions. There had been many of her kind in the shop at one time. She had cream-coloured silky fur which she was constantly grooming.

'Where are they now? And what will happen to us?' she would ask.

'Better not to ask,' Skip, the brown rabbit, advised, 'as none of us has the answer.'

'Perhaps they've gone to the windmill,' said Thrifty, the golden hamster.

'Don't be absurd,' said Pie, the sleek black-and-white rat, scornfully. 'They were taken, like all of us will be taken eventually.' He sat up and washed his whiskers.

'I won't be taken! Not me!' shrieked Auntie, the grey parrot, sidling along her perch and dipping her head at the little animal. 'HELLO AUNTIE. HERE'S A NUT. HELLO AUNTIE. HERE'S A NUT. HERE YOU ARE OLD GIRL. HERE YOU ARE.' She mimicked Dobson's speech in her shrill voice as if to reinforce her assertion.

The mock human sounds always confused the animals. They would sit quite still, fascinated yet puzzled, waiting for Dobson to appear. They recognized the self-same sounds that came from his mouth. If he didn't appear they felt almost as though they had been tricked. Spider would clamber to the side of his cage that faced Auntie and, gripping the mesh with his hands and feet, would stare at the bird for minutes at a time without moving. Auntie stared back, rocking her head from side to side and hugging her mystery to herself. Spider's great intelligence and near-human attributes were quite unable to deal with this situation – even to find a clue. Auntie had them all baffled. Only Pebble, who was not very susceptible to the sounds of human speech and whose hearing was not the sharpest, anyway, avoided being fooled.

The shop opened at half-past nine. Eric arrived at nine o'clock. He replaced the stale food in the cages with fresh. If he had time, he tidied the animals' containers and cleaned where necessary. Mr Dobson tried to hurry him, reminding him all the while of opening hours as if he expected a flood of customers to pour through the door the moment it was unlocked. Eric muttered impolite remarks under his breath.

The first customer rarely appeared before ten o'clock. Two or three might follow but it was a trickle, not a flood. Sometimes customers were so sparse you couldn't even have called them a trickle; more a drip.

*

One day a woman came in with her young daughter who was entranced by Skip and begged her mother to buy him. Her mother was doubtful. The child already had a menagerie of animals. But she didn't have a rabbit and she pleaded incessantly.

'Please, please, Mummy. He's so sweet. Look at the way he hops about. And he's got such lovely eyes.'

Her mother wavered. Joel Dobson, who always dealt with the sale of livestock himself, hovered nearby. But he didn't do anything to urge the sale – Skip was his last rabbit and he didn't want him to go. He had given him his name – just as he had given names to all the others in the shop, the last of their kind. He really hoped the mother would stand firm. But the child was so insistent the mother at last succumbed.

'All right, all right, Chrissie.' She turned to the proprietor. 'How much is he?'

'Er – that one?' queried Dobson, as if there were a dozen to choose from. 'That one's not for sale, I'm afraid.'

The child looked upset. Eric stood open-mouthed.

'Oh, I see,' said the woman, relieved to have the decision taken for her. 'I'm sorry, Chrissie. Now never mind, dear.' Tears were imminent.

'Wh-what about *him*?' the child whispered, pointing to Candyfloss.

'It's a "her", actually,' Dobson replied, smiling. 'And the same thing applies.'

The child began to sob. The mother gathered up her purchases and hastened the little girl away. She felt there might be a scene.

Eric strode over. 'Why did you say that?' he demanded of the old man. 'Of course they're for sale. Why else are they here?'

Dobson shrugged. 'I decide what's for sale in my own shop,' he answered coolly.

'But – but. . . .' Eric spluttered angrily.

'No "buts",' said Dobson. 'I just didn't feel like letting them go, that's all.'

'That's unfair; and cruel!' Eric shouted, his anger getting the better of him. 'You can't keep them for ever in those poky boxes.'

'I can do what I like,' Dobson reminded him.

'I-I'll. . . .'

'You'll what?' snapped the old man.

Eric backed down and marched away, cursing silently. He thought the man should be taught a lesson. It was obvious he meant to keep these few creatures in their cramped quarters indefinitely. A wicked idea came into Eric's head and he smiled inwardly. It was for the sake of the animals, he told himself. And he began to devise a plan.

The first thing to arrange was a period when he could be alone in the shop after hours. This would be difficult. Joel Dobson was very particular about times and kept to a regular routine. At five-thirty the shop closed and Dobson expected Eric to finish off any jobs and be on his way by six. The old man then went up to his flat to cook himself a light meal. What pretext could Eric use to stay late? And would Dobson allow him to remain on the premises alone? The young man (he was eighteen and only a 'boy' in the animals' understanding) decided there was one way in which he might be granted the facility. He

11

would offer to do some unpaid over-time. The suggestion might well appeal to the shop owner's love of economy. Eric made up his mind to put it to the test.

The next day Eric mentioned the idea. Dobson was taken aback, if not actually suspicious.

'What's so pressing that it needs to be done in the evening?' he queried.

There was only the one feasible answer. 'I thought I'd clean the pens and containers out.'

'Oh, you and this cleaning!' the old man exclaimed impatiently. 'You think of nothing else.'

'Well, if you won't let me do it during the day. . . .'

Dobson muttered something which Eric failed to catch.

'It's for the animals' benefit,' he continued persuasively. 'And if you mean to keep them here for—'

'For what?' the old man cut in. 'For as long as I choose, yes,' he answered himself. 'All right, then,' he went on, 'if you're *so* keen. When do you want to do it?'

'This evening's as good as any time.'

'No, that's no good. There's something on TV I want to catch at seven o'clock.'

'I wouldn't interrupt you.'

'You don't think I'm going to leave you here in my shop on your own, do you? Prowling about and upsetting things!'

Eric was riled by the accusation. 'What do you mean, upsetting things?' he demanded. '*I'm* the one

12

who's always tidying up. And if you don't trust me,' he added daringly, 'why do you employ me?'

Dobson apparently accepted this as fair comment. 'Very well. Have it your own way. But you said "unpaid" so don't come running to me later with any sort of demand. I haven't asked you to do it.'

'I shan't coming running to you for anything,' Eric assured him sullenly. 'I'll do what I want to do – and go.' Mentally he was hugging himself. No more was said on the subject.

That evening Dobson hung about for as long as he could while Eric got busy. The old man stood and watched and occasionally gave voice to unnecessary directions. Eric gritted his teeth and ignored him, moving from one cage to another. At last he said, innocently enough, 'Aren't you going to get something to eat?'

Dobson grunted. 'In a minute, in a minute. How long d'you think you'll be?'

'About another hour. That should finish it.'

'Well, you must want something to do, that's all I can say.' Joel Dobson turned to go. 'Shout up when you're through,' he called over his shoulder, 'and I'll come and unlock the door.'

Eric thought swiftly. Here was a problem. He needed the door open now if he was to carry out his plan. 'Oh – er – couldn't you do that now?' he asked, trying to sound nonchalant. 'Then I won't have to disturb you.'

'What! And leave the shop open for anyone to walk in?' the old man cried. 'Don't be ridiculous!' He came trudging back.

13

'I shall be here, won't I?' Eric reminded him irritably.

The two glared at each other. Then Eric had a brainwave. 'I might need to empty the bucket in the street before I'm done,' he hazarded.

Dobson sighed. '*Very* well,' he growled and stamped over to the door. He unlocked it.

'Keep your eye on it,' he warned Eric. 'And you'll still need to call up afterwards so that I can come down and lock it up again. Don't forget.'

'Of course I won't forget.'

'All right then.'

Eric heaved a sigh of relief as the old man disappeared. He wasted no more than another quarter of an hour cleaning; just long enough to make sure Dobson was safely occupied upstairs. Then he went to the door and peered through the glass. The hilly street was deserted. He opened the door silently and wedged it with the usual slab of rubber. Then he went to the cages and stealthily, carefully, lifted out the animals and placed them on the floor. Pebble immediately retreated into his shell. Pie, Thrifty, Skip and Candyfloss ran uncertainly around the shop, bumping into each other and becoming panicky. None of them headed for the open doorway. With thumping heart, Eric released the catch on Spider's cage and flung the metal gate wide. The monkey jumped down from a rung and stood on the threshold as if scenting liberty. But he made no move. Eric waited nervously. The hamster and the rat were trying to climb amongst some boxes. Their instinct was to hide away. The presence of the boy, towering

14

over them without the reassuring screen of their cage sides between him and them, was very alarming.

Spider hesitated a while longer, then swung out of his cage on to the floor, picking up a fragment of fruit, thoughtfully. The animals' reaction to freedom was not at all what Eric had expected. He realized he had been naive. He strode to the doorway and looked out. There was no traffic, no passers-by. Now he decided to aid the animals in their flight. He looked across the street at where the fields began and then came quickly back. He grabbed the hamster in one hand and the rat in the other and carried the struggling little bodies outside and over the road, setting them down by the fence on the edge of the first field. It was not a close-boarded fence and Pie soon found a gap and disappeared. Thrifty started to run along the pavement. Eric had to push her, physically, into the long grass. Now he ran back for the others.

Pebble had emerged from his shell and his scaly head was slowly turning as he looked at his strange new surroundings. Eric lifted him and carried him out to join the others.

As he returned a second time, Skip bolted through the doorway and, scenting the vegetation beyond, bounded across the road and squeezed through the fence. Eric smiled. Candyfloss showed no desire to leave at all. Spider was near the open door, sniffing at the air. Eric picked up Candyfloss, crossed to the field and called Spider's name. The guinea pig was made to follow her companions. Spider ran over to Eric and looked up at him expectantly. The monkey thought he was to be rewarded with a titbit. Eric hoisted him over the fence, then ran back to the shop.

15

Auntie, the grey parrot, had shifted on her perch to watch the comings and goings. Eric came into the shop to see Auntie staring at him with a look that he imagined to be one of condemnation. He had clean forgotten her. He went to release her. Then he remembered the chain. She was fastened to the perch!

'HELLO AUNTIE. GOOD OLD GIRL,' said the parrot.

Eric bent to examine the chain. It was fitted in a loop around one of her legs. He tried to lift the leg to see how the loop clipped. Auntie squawked. Eric paused, listening for sounds upstairs. Nothing. He realized he must hurry before Auntie made too much noise. He clutched at her leg. Auntie flapped her wings in fright, making a loud clattering. Eric hung on. He saw the clip was a pincer type like on a dog's lead and struggled to unloose it. Auntie screeched and, as she beat her wings, the chain came away. She found herself flying round the shop. But where was her owner? She was terrified. Eric was ready for flight too. The din the parrot was making was tremendous.

'Shoo! Shoo!' he cried, trying to drive her out of the shop. But Auntie didn't want to leave; she just wanted to get away from the boy who had suddenly become a threat. Upstairs, Joel Dobson heard the frightened squawks and was coming to investigate. Eric bolted. As the old man reached the ground floor his approach made the unreasoning bird more panicky than ever. She saw one way out of the terrifying situation and flew through the doorway just as Dobson arrived. He saw her sail high over the road and up into a lofty branch of a sycamore where she perched, shrieking at the top of her voice.

The Windmill Pet Shop was pet-less.

——— 3 ———

Outside the Shop

Joel Dobson paused on the threshold of his shop. To his left, Eric was pelting downhill as fast as his legs would carry him. To his right Auntie, the grey parrot, shifted restlessly on the sycamore branch. She had stopped shrieking and was beginning a repertoire of noises reminiscent of a battery of corks being pulled from a large collection of wine bottles.

'Auntie! Auntie! Come down,' Dobson called to her plaintively. Of the escaped pets, she alone was visible.

Auntie turned her head to one side. 'HELLO AUNTIE. LOVELY MORNING,' she said as she sat in the September evening sunshine.

Dobson sighed. Silly bird! He leant against the door frame feeling hurt and baffled. How could Eric have been so vindictive? He had never done him any harm. Now, for the first time in all these years, the shop was empty of life. He felt he didn't want to go back into it. It was gloomy and unwelcoming. It seemed pointless carrying on with it. But wasn't that what he had wanted – the excuse to finish with it? Dobson shook his head. No, not like this. He had wanted to bring himself to this point in his own time,

17

not to have it forced upon him. His mind was full of contradictory notions. For, despite himself, it seemed as if a weight had been taken off his shoulders.

All at once the reality of the situation gripped him. How would the animals manage? Turned out into a hostile and dangerous world they knew nothing of, they would soon come to grief. Spider, in particular, was vulnerable. He wouldn't even be able to adapt to the climate. And his owner had left him in care! Dobson shuddered. He shook himself and sprang into action. He must search for them!

It was obvious none of the animals were in the street. He strode to the field edge and, ignoring Auntie for the moment, began to scan the immediate area for any signs of life.

'HERE'S A NUT, AUNTIE. HERE'S A NUT,' squawked the parrot.

The animals, in fact, had not gone very far. They had been plunged into liberty unwittingly – not in the usual way, singly, in the arms or basket of a shop customer. They had not expected this sort of release, and it was a while before they could come to terms with it. But, once they realized they were free, they began to feel more confident. Well – most of them did, and these urged the others on.

Amongst the long grass and bushes Spider was the most conspicuous. He was eager to move farther on. 'Remember the windmill!' he cried as he bounded away. 'I'll meet you there!' But, before long, he found it necessary to stop and raise himself on his hind legs to look around and get his bearings. He had left the others far behind.

Pie and Thrifty, the two smallest, were well hidden. They stuck together for comfort. Pie was the bolder of the two. 'Come on,' he squeaked to his old neighbour from the shop. 'They'll be looking for us.' He made no distinction between the boy and the man, even though it had been the boy who had released them. Humans were all one to him. The boy had emerged victorious but now Pie suspected he had some scheme of his own. Thrifty followed the black-and-white rat closely.

'I wish they *would* look for us,' Candyfloss remarked to Skip. She wanted nothing else than to get back to the security and familiarity of the shop. She was running around in circles, unable to pause long enough to think which was the best way back.

'*I* don't,' declared Skip. 'Can't you smell those delicious aromas? They're all around us. I can't wait to sample some of these juicy plants.'

The timid Candyfloss wasn't interested. She'd never felt less like eating. How typical of Skip to be thinking of his stomach! She had shared a cage with him long enough to know all about his chief interest in life. She ran into Pebble who was blundering on at his snail's pace through the grass and was quite undiverted by her nervousness. He liked to travel in a straight line.

'Where are you going, Pebble?' shrilled the guinea pig. 'How can you know where you're going?'

'I'll know when I get there,' he muttered drily and went on past.

Candyfloss noticed a fencepost and thought she recognized it. She headed towards it. Through the gaps in the palings she could see the road and, across

19

that, the shop. She had never seen the shop from outside before and, had the door not been open, the guinea pig wouldn't have known what she was looking at. But, through the doorway, she saw the cages, the pens, the tanks; the clutter she had seen every day of her life. 'Skip!' she called excitedly. 'I can see it! I can see home!' Her words were lost. Skip had loped off and was nibbling some dandelion leaves with every appearance of relish.

'POP! POP! POP! POP!' Auntie's cork noises died away and she followed them with a perfect imitation of the pet-shop telephone. 'HELLO. WINDMILL PET SHOP.' She answered her own ringing tone.

Candyfloss stopped, hearing the tones of the shop owner. She looked around, expecting to see him.

'SHUT UP AUNTIE. NO MORE NUTS,' shrieked the parrot.

Dobson bent and scooped Candyfloss into his arms. He hadn't uttered a word, but Auntie had brought the first of the animals safely back. The old man whispered a 'thank you' to the bird and hurried the guinea pig into the shop. Candyfloss's period of freedom had been short-lived indeed.

Dobson returned to the field, wondering if Auntie might have decoyed any of the other pets within his reach. He could see no sign as yet. But, he reasoned, the parrot could be useful to him if he allowed her to remain in the open. He had a feeling the animals might be drawn by her 'human' calls. He could see she had all her favourite foods, of course. It would be easy to leave them in a convenient spot for her. And as long as the weather stayed fine. . . .

*

However, for the rest of that evening there were no more successes. Auntie had decided she had done enough impersonations for one day and she fell silent. Dobson brought her fruit, greenery and a pot of water, all of which he contrived to hang from the lower branches of the sycamore. But the pet shop door closed that night on Candyfloss alone. The guinea pig, tucked into her nest of straw, with no Skip to accompany her, wondered when the others would return and knew she had been too hasty in her desire for safety.

—4—

Mischief Maker

Auntie was nowhere to be seen in the morning. Her food was gone and so was she. Needless to say, Eric was not to be seen either. Dobson had not expected to see him. He didn't bother with ringing his home. He thought it unlikely they would meet again even though there were some wages owed.

The old man didn't open the shop that day. He spent quite a while tending Candyfloss. She was precious to him now. Then he set off in search of the others.

The night had been a frightening experience for the animals. Strange noises and strange smells had come to threaten their freedom. Pie and Thrifty had hidden themselves in a grass tussock. The hamster had stuffed her cheek pouches with berries which she'd gathered on the move. She had been obsessed with the idea of storing food and this had impeded their progress.

The rabbit had eaten many new varieties of vegetation. But when darkness came Skip, replete, had missed his old companion and sought the company of the smaller animals. He hadn't found them and he'd spent an uneasy night, dozing and waking at every rustle in the undergrowth. In the gathering daylight he began to look for them again. None of the animals, except Spider, had gone beyond the first field.

The monkey had spent the night in a tree. He'd wedged himself in the fork of a lime tree in a patch of woodland dividing two fields. His grey-brown body was perfectly camouflaged against the branches and he draped his limbs over the branch as he enjoyed an untroubled sleep in the warm night air. The next morning he awoke hungry and set about finding food. He caught insects on the trunk and branches of the tree with his nimble fingers but they weren't sufficient to satisfy him. He swung down from the tree, his long arms reaching branch after branch with ease until he was on the floor of the wood. There were titbits to be found amongst the leaf litter; tasty millipedes, woodlice and beetles which Spider crammed eagerly into his mouth. But they seemed only to irritate his appetite. The monkey screwed up his already screwed-up little face even more and chattered to himself. He wanted fruit and vegetables. A blackbird peered at him through the branches with great curiosity. It had never seen anything like Spider before. The monkey, who was imagining he was eating the sweetest, most succulent fruits, turned his face towards the bird which flapped away, uttering cries of alarm. 'Pink! Pink! Pink!'

Spider watched it with his habitually bemused expression. 'Fruit,' he said to himself, returning to more important matters. 'Fruit.' And he started to think where he could get some. There was certainly none to be had amongst these trees. He walked slowly along the ground on all fours in a meditative sort of way. He was a compact, four-square little figure. He laid his long fingers and toes flat at each step. Spider recalled Eric and old Dobson; he equated the provision of fruit with humans. It was because of this that he decided to look for signs of his distant cousins. He increased his pace to a bounding run and came out of the woods into the second field. At the edge of this field was a cottage with a long garden. Spider heard human sounds and headed in their direction. The garden was enclosed by a clipped hedge. This was no barrier to him. He balanced himself on its flat top to take stock of the situation.

Two women were in the garden, close to the house. One was pegging washing to a line, the other sat in a garden chair. Spider saw the people and he grinned a monkey grin at them. He also saw an apple tree laden with fruit at one end of the garden. They were red apples and Spider smelt their sweetness. He wasted no time. It was only a short hop to the ground, then away he raced for the tree. He wasn't noticed at first as he bounded over the long lawn. The woman in the chair, who was elderly, was dozing in the sun, whilst the other was concentrating on her task. Spider leapt into the apple tree and scampered up the boughs. His keen eyes picked out the reddest apples. Eagerly he began to snap off the rosy fruit with one hand, gathering them into the crook of his opposite arm. He took a bite from them here and there as he picked them. The apples were crisp and juicy. Spider uttered grunts of pleasure.

Eventually the younger woman detected movement out of the corner of her eye. Her head swivelled round, a couple of clothes pegs clamped between her teeth. She saw the monkey in her apple tree and gaped. The pegs dropped to the ground.

'Loo-look, Mother!' she stammered, scarcely able to believe her eyes. 'A monkey!'

The old lady awoke with a start. 'What! What did you say?'

Her daughter pointed wordlessly to the apple tree. Spider had heard their voices and was regarding them tentatively. He clutched his collection of fruit in his left arm and made a surreptitious movement for another apple, his eyes still on the woman. He didn't trust humans. It was not that he disliked them. But, in Spider's experience, the one human priority seemed to be to stop you doing what you really wanted to do.

'He's pinching the apples,' the old lady said, needlessly.

'Where *could* he have come from?' muttered her daughter. 'He's escaped from somewhere, that's obvious.'

'There's no one round here with a pet monkey.'

'Perhaps he's got a name tag. We'd better have a look.'

The two women advanced down the lawn. Spider froze. As they came nearer he reacted instinctively and climbed higher into the tree. He clutched his apples so tightly that some of them popped from his grasp and bounced down to the grass. Spider chattered down angrily at the human figures.

'We'll never get to him up there,' remarked the old lady.

Spider seemed to realize he was safe and took some refreshing bites from one of the remaining apples. He chewed contemplatively.

'What a cheeky expression,' said the young woman, shading her eyes as she gazed up at him. 'You can't help laughing.'

The old lady wasn't amused. 'Someone's not doing their job properly,' she contended, 'letting an animal like that get out! You can see it's wild.'

'Oh, Mum, he's only small,' said her daughter. 'I'm sure he's quite harmless.'

'Well, we can't just leave him there, can we?'

'He's not doing a lot of damage.'

'What about your apples, Tina? What will Nicholas say?'

'I don't think one little monkey, who must be hungry, will bother Nicholas very much. He's nuts about animals anyway. It's a pity, really, he's not here to see it.'

Spider continued to munch his apples. He sensed the two women posed no threat to him. Gradually his appetite eased. He looked around him. The women had returned to the other end of the garden. The washing was stretched on the line, barely moving in the slight breeze. Spider knew he was still being watched and wondered what the humans would do next. The minutes passed and nothing happened. The younger woman had taken a seat next to her mother. Even the family cat was asleep in a sunny spot under the hedge. Spider grew bored; he decided to amuse himself. He held a half-eaten apple in his hand, stood up, carefully balancing himself on his branch, and hurled the unwanted fruit at the unsuspecting black-and-white cat. The apple failed to hit the animal but it landed nearby with a thud and bounced into the hedge. The cat jumped up and ran on to the lawn, not knowing the cause of its alarm. Spider jumped up and down, chattering excitedly. He had discovered a good game. Taking his last remaining apple from his other arm he threw it with some force at the unsettled cat. The fruit went bowling along the grass, setting the cat racing for the safety of the cottage, and came to rest abruptly against a leg of the old woman's chair.

'Look at that now, Tina!' she exclaimed. 'He's a mischievous little creature. He's frightened poor Tom half to death!'

Spider's game wasn't over just because the cat had disappeared. He was having great fun and just getting into his stride. Now he started to pluck apples from the tree indiscriminately, all of which he sent with surprising accuracy in the direction of the old woman.

'Stop him, Tina!' she cried. 'He's pelting me!'

Tina jumped up and, taking care to avoid the hail of missiles, ran round to the tree. She clapped her hands loudly. 'Now then, that's enough!'

Spider was startled and swung from his perch to a lower branch. The tree wasn't very tall and the young woman made a lunge for him. Spider evaded her and jumped to the ground. Tina tried to catch him. Spider looked around for another tree as she gave chase. There wasn't one in sight. The only safe high point he could see was the washing line. He bounded across the grass and scrambled up the line prop. Grabbing the line, he swung along it, legs dangling, with all the accomplishment of a trapeze artist. Shirts threatened to envelop him but he pulled himself clear. However, a large sheet finally got the better of him and entangled him completely.

'Quick, Mum, catch hold of him!' called Tina.

'What? *I* can't touch him,' the old lady answered distastefully.

'Oh, really!' Her daughter ran up and flung her arms round the wriggling Spider who was now cocooned like an Egyptian mummy in about two metres of white cotton. She carried the bundle hastily indoors, shutting the door behind her. She glanced about for a container large enough to hold the struggling monkey. The only thing that was remotely big enough was the empty linen basket. Tina whipped off the lid with one hand and stuffed Spider, sheet and all inside. Then she slammed the lid on the top. Spider's muffled gibberings could be heard coming forlornly from the receptacle.

'It's all right, Mum!' Tina yelled. 'He's safe now. You can come in, if you like.' She opened the door.

Spider was wrestling manfully with the sheet and had succeeded in getting his head clear. The wicker basket rocked with his efforts. Tom, the cat, eyed this strange phenomenon with misgiving. His tail swished nervously. He was ready to fly again at the drop of a hat. As the old lady came into the kitchen, the linen basket tipped over, spilling its live contents at her feet. Tom fled. Spider, trailing the sheet behind him like a rather unfaancy sort of wedding train, vanished into the garden. The sheet fell away and the monkey raced for the hedge. He was up and over in a trice, leaving the garden and his first encounter with the local human population well behind him.

Spider ran for a while and then paused to take stock. He had not been frightened by his encounter and in fact had rather enjoyed the escapade. He was no longer hungry and his games with the apples and the washing line had only been marred by his temporary smothering by the sheet. He decided there was plenty of scope for adventure amongst humans and their possessions, but he made up his mind never to allow himself to come close enough to be captured in future. Now he remembered the windmill and he stood on his hind legs and looked into the distance. From the ground he could see its black shape on the horizon but he wanted a clearer view. He headed back to the patch of woodland and climbed to the top of a very tall tree. It was while he was gazing at the well-known landmark he had seen every day from the pet shop-window that he heard the voice of the shop owner.

'THAT'S IT. THAT'S IT. TAKE ANOTHER GRAPE.'

He looked all around for Joel Dobson, chattering expectantly as he did so. The man was nowhere to be seen but, with a clatter of her grey wings, Auntie landed in a neighbouring tree.

'It's you!' cried Spider. He was rather pleased to see the old parrot. 'Where have you been?'

'There and back again,' Auntie informed him cryptically. 'The door was closed.'

'What door?' Spider asked, baring his yellow teeth at her in a gesture of friendship.

'*Our* door, of course.' Auntie stared at him with her yellow-ringed dark eyes.

29

'You've been back to the shop?'

'Certainly. Where else should I go?'

'But, that life's all over now, isn't it? We have to make for the windmill.'

'Oh, you animals and the windmill! What do you think you'll find there?'

'You'll understand when you arrive. We were all to meet at the windmill, that was the idea.'

'Well, *I* want feeding. The man left me some food last night but he hasn't been back. So that means we're to go back to the shop for it.'

'Of course it doesn't, of course it doesn't, silly parrot,' Spider gibbered irritably. 'How can we if the door's closed?'

Auntie was flummoxed. 'Then what . . .' she faltered.

'I told you. That life's over,' Spider repeated. 'Now we feed ourselves.'

'With what?' Auntie screeched. 'I don't see any grapes or bananas or nuts or – anything.'

'It's easy,' Spider told her with an air of superiority. 'I've already done it. You have to look for it. And when you find it, you just take it.'

'Mischief maker,' said Auntie.

'Oh no. No mischief in feeding ourselves,' said Spider slyly. 'Do you want me to show you how? Are you hungry?'

'Yes, I'm hungry. POP! POP!' Auntie pulled a couple of corks.

'Come on, then. We'll go together.' Spider grinned. This was going to be fun.

—— 5 ——

More Antics

Pie and Thrifty, that same morning, shared a convivial nibble at the hamster's hoard of berries before they left their shelter of the night.

'Is it safe to move, Pie?' the hamster asked nervously.

Pie's whiskers twitched busily. 'Far as I can tell, yes. No strange noises in the daytime, eh? Nothing alarming anyway. We can't stay here, Thrifty.'

'I don't want to stay here,' she returned. 'But we're so tiny and it's such a big world.'

'I'll look after you,' Pie said gallantly. 'And, if we're so tiny, who's going to bother with us?'

They pulled themselves out of the grass tussock and, running swiftly on their agile little feet, began to thread their way through the tall stalks in the field. They would have been hard to spot by any creature in search of them, so well screened were they. So Skip could find no trace of them, try as he might.

The rabbit did bump into Pebble, however, as he ran the length and breadth of the field. He was quite relieved. 'Oh, I'm glad I've found one of you,' he said breathlessly. 'I've been looking for the others. Have you seen them?'

'Haven't seen anybody,' said Pebble abruptly. 'Except you.'

'I don't like being on my own,' Skip confessed. 'Candyfloss left me and – and – I'd like your company.'

'You can have it,' said Pebble, 'but are you sure you really want it? You'd soon tire of me, I think. I can't keep up with you.'

Skip was nonplussed. 'Well, I – er – I'll try and keep up with *you*,' he offered.

'Not natural for a fleet-footed creature like a rabbit to move at my pace,' Pebble warned. 'You'd do better to leave me to make my own way. It's very kind of you, of course. But I can't bear rushing anywhere. I'm afraid we'd soon fall out.'

'Oh dear,' said Skip. 'Perhaps you're right. We'll meet again, though, won't we, at the windmill?'

'Of course we will,' said Pebble. 'I'll try and get there before the winter. Otherwise I shall have to hibernate.'

Skip gulped. Winter? Hibernate? But it was still summer now! He couldn't comprehend such extreme leisureliness. 'I see what you mean about rushing,' he ventured. 'Look, Pebble, if you see Pie or Thrifty or Spider tell them I've been searching for them and – and – to look out for me.'

'All right,' Pebble agreed, 'but there's very little chance of it. You see how I am.'

Skip did see. The tortoise had barely covered ten metres across the field since he had been released. 'Goo-goodbye then,' he said hurriedly. 'Till the windmill!' He loped off, still marvelling at the reptile's snail's pace.

The field sloped downhill to the little wooded patch where Spider had spent the night. Skip reached the wood before the smaller animals, although he didn't come across them on the way. The tall trees cast a deep shade. Skip entered the dim interior warily. The sunlight shining on the next field beyond beckoned him on. His brown body was inconspicuous on the leafy floor, but his white powder-puff tail was like a beacon in the gloom.

At a distance Spider saw the flash of white. He and Auntie were sitting together on a branch eating blackberries. The monkey had gathered them from a bramble bush and had scratched himself badly. He wasn't in a good mood. He knew that the animal now approaching, loping this way and that, was Skip, but he gave no sign. He wanted to be the first at the windmill and didn't want Skip to overtake him. He sat quite still.

Auntie took a blackberry from the diminishing pile with her usual daintiness, her grey beak and tongue working together to separate the berry she had chosen from the others. Skip came closer. Auntie saw the rabbit. 'Skip!' she squawked. 'Skip! POP! POP!'

The rabbit froze and looked upwards. Spider gibbered irritably at the parrot. Auntie turned her head on one side. 'HELLO AUNTIE. GOOD MORNING,' She said.

Skip looked round hastily. 'Quick, hide,' he called to Spider. 'The master's coming!'

'He's *not* coming,' cried Spider crossly. 'Auntie's playing games. You go on, Skip. We'll catch you up. We've some food up here to eat. Then we'll come.'

The rabbit hesitated. 'I'll wait,' he said. 'I'm in no hurry.'

'No, no,' Spider answered. 'We don't want you to wait. That's not the idea at all. You're supposed to go on – to the windmill.'

'I know, I know. But can't we go together? I mean—'

'No, we can't all bunch together like a – a – pet shop on legs,' Spider finished. 'We'd be noticed. Go on. We shan't be far behind.'

Skip was suspicious. Was Spider hatching a scheme? But he wasn't an animal to stay around when he wasn't wanted. 'Oh very well. Suit yourself,' he said. 'But if you see Pie or Thrifty—'

'We *won't* see them,' Spider told him bluntly. 'We're going our own way.'

'D'YOU WANT A BIT OF BISCUIT?' queried Auntie.

Spider rounded on her. 'Do shut up,' he said. 'Or use your own voice!'

Auntie replied with a perfect imitation of a lavatory flushing. It was so realistic that Spider nearly fell from his perch. Skip vanished. He'd always thought there was something distinctly odd about the parrot.

Pie and Thrifty made heavy going through the jungle of grass-stalks. They were glad to reach the wood. Spider and Auntie had by then long vacated the area. The wood seemed deserted. Thrifty found some blackberries underneath the tree where the two had settled and she stowed them automatically into her cheek pouches. They stuck out on either side of her head making her look like the hamster equivalent of a prize fighter with over-developed shoulders.

'Weighing yourself down again?' Pie commented.

'Never know when they might come in useful,' Thrifty answered.

'Maybe, but you look quite top heavy to me.'

'I won't hold us up if that's what you're worried about.'

They scurried on through the rustling leaves. Pie's sensitive nose picked out a thousand different scents.

'Funny we've seen nothing of the others,' Thrifty remarked.

'We will do,' the rat replied. 'They've been this way.'

'We must be last then?'

'Never,' declared Pie. 'Not while old Pebble's behind us. He's so slow, a beetle could outpace him. But what do you mean "last" anyway? We're not in a race, are we?'

'I think it may develop into one.'

'Why should it?'

'I don't know. But I have a feeling there's something about the windmill. There's something there. . . .' Her voice petered out.

'Something there?'

'Yes, something Spider knows about. He could always see more from his cage than we could and he's so clever.'

'Is he now? We'll see about that.' Pie's competitive instinct was aroused. He put on a spurt.

'It's no good trying to overtake him,' Thrifty called from behind. 'He could always outrun us.'

'But he may not know the best route,' Pie observed

35

subtly. 'There'll be many an obstacle before we get there.'

Spider and Auntie had all the time in the world for diversions. Auntie wanted to fly all the way to the windmill and see just what was there, but Spider told her there was no need; they'd reach it all in good time and meanwhile they may as well have some fun on the way.

The blackberries hadn't lasted them very long. Auntie was hungry again and Spider was keen to show her his prowess at making capital out of humans. 'They'll provide for us,' he told her. 'You'll see.'

They crossed the second field, Spider bounding through the grass and the grey parrot flying a little ahead and then alighting periodically to allow him to catch up. By a roundabout route, as they looked for signs of human habitation, they brought themselves in sight of the centre of the town of Wandle. The noise and bustle of the streets attracted Spider like a magnet. He ran towards it. Auntie flew up to perch on a telegraph pole where she sat, shrieking in excitement. She had seen a greengrocer's stall with its multicoloured wares. The rich heady aroma of ripe fruit wafted to her on the breeze. She forgot all about the monkey. With a clatter of wings she swooped down amongst the astonished shoppers, pounced on a purple plum in the midst of an artistically arranged pyramid of fruit and flapped away to a lamp post to enjoy it. The pile of plums, so neatly balanced before, collapsed entirely and the fruit went cascading from the stall all over the pavement. Startled customers unwittingly squashed the plums underfoot as they milled about, astounded at the bird's audacity.

'Hey, you little pest, come here!' roared the vendor, grabbing a broom from the side of his stall and angrily trying to knock Auntie from her perch with it. But she was far too high up and, with the most admirable calmness, pecked fragments from the ripe plum which she held down by one claw. The human hubbub increased. Some people were beginning to titter. The greengrocer was furious and tried to rescue what fruit he could from the jostling on-lookers. Auntie continued to enjoy her fruit and, when she had finished, nonchalantly dropped the plum-stone into the gutter. She turned her head on one side and watched the gathering with her beady eyes.

'ALL GONE. ALL GONE. HAVE A NUT,' she squawked pensively.

The crowd roared. Auntie eyed the display of fruit. She was selecting her next titbit. The greengrocer was still on his hands and knees, calling on the shoppers in vain to give him some space. Auntie fluttered down and, with all the expertise of a quality controller, selected the largest strawberry she could find, seized it with her hooked beak and regained her perch above the heads of the crowd. She placed it under one foot.

'POP! POP!' She drew some corks, preparatory to settling down to enjoy her second course.

There was quite a gathering by now around the lamp post. More passers-by stopped to swell the numbers. Auntie ate the strawberry with great delicacy, savouring her audience. And now on to the scene, attracted by the cries and laughter, came a second entertainer determined to steal the limelight. It was, of course, Spider who was feeling in his most mischievous mood.

The monkey shinned halfway up the lamp post where he swung effortlessly by one arm and grinned at the throng like a clown about to embark on his act. Then he climbed swiftly to the top and made as if to grab Auntie's strawberry. Auntie, however, had no intention of giving it up. She swung her head round and pecked Spider quite savagely on his finger. Spider screamed and jumped up and down as if he had been stung, only narrowly avoiding losing his balance on the arm of the lamp post. The human audience could hardly believe what they were seeing. They looked around, scanning faces in the mêlée for the perpetrator of this free show. Needless to say, no one identified himself. By now the greengrocer was on his feet again. Spider continued to scream, not in pain but in anger at Auntie's attack.

'Give him a banana,' someone suggested playfully. 'That'll quieten him down.'

Auntie finished her strawberry and, with a look of distaste at the noisy monkey, flew off to a quieter spot on a rooftop. Spider immediately fell silent. He was aware that he had succeeded in driving off his rival for the attention of the crowd. He looked at the sea of faces below, as if weighing up how best to create an impression. The greengrocer watched the monkey with a keener anticipation even than the amused onlookers. He was wondering what pranks Spider was planning at his expense.

Some of the other members of the crowd adopted the suggestion of the bananas.

'Go on, you can spare one. He looks hungry,' a man urged the unfortunate greengrocer.

'You must be joking,' the stall owner growled. 'What's going on? It's a ruddy zoo! Someone's going to pay—' His voice was drowned by a new surge of laughter as Spider decided to take matters into his own hands. He clambered some way down the lamp post and then leapt recklessly out into space, landing plumb on top of the greengrocer's shoulders. Grasping the man's neck with one hand for support, Spider leant down and snatched a bunch of the very bananas the crowd had been wishing on him. Bananas were indeed one of Spider's favourite foods and now, still clutching the fruit purveyor's neck in a firm but none-too-friendly grip, he proceeded to peel the largest in the bunch he was clutching, using teeth and fingers.

'Get off me!' the greengrocer shouted, wriggling and striking out at the monkey on his back. He was tired of being the butt of the crowd's humour and was absolutely livid. However, Spider avoided the blows and clung on.

At the back of the crowd, eyes popping, red-haired Eric was gaping at the antics of the monkey whose performance in Wandle High Street had only been made possible by his own actions the previous day. The youth didn't know whether to feel embarrassed or delighted. Either way he did feel responsible and he cast surreptitious glances up and down the street to see if Joel Dobson was in the vicinity. But the old man was in quite another quarter, combing the neighbouring fields for his lost pets.

The greengrocer finally succeeded, with a vicious twist, in dislodging his uninvited piggy-back. Spider jumped to the pavement shrieking and, bananas intact, rushed across the road. The crowd gave a great gasp as a van screeched to a halt with only a metre to spare. Eric made an involuntary lurch but Spider was safely across and now bounded on three legs down the opposite side of the road, dodging shoppers and with his bananas pressed firmly to his chest.

Auntie cackled from the roof top as she saw him racing away and the next minute she was besieged by a horde of house-martins whose mud nests were under the eaves of the roof on which she had settled. The large grey bird was an alien amongst them and they dive-bombed this threat to their nestlings, squealing as they buffeted her, then wheeling away to dart back a second time.

'GOOD MORNING. WINDMILL PET SHOP,' Auntie ventured. But the fierce little birds were having none of it and continued their attack. Auntie ducked and weaved but eventually succumbed, flapping away with a puzzled squawk in the direction Spider had taken. Wandle High Street returned to normality and the monkey and parrot returned to the less stimulating environment of the surrounding countryside.

—— 6 ——

To the Windmill

Joel Dobson sought in earnest for his missing animals. He was particularly concerned about Spider who didn't belong to him anyway and he felt he had an obligation to find him on the owner's behalf. His friend, a retired military man, had entrusted the monkey to him and now, thanks to that foolish boy Eric, Spider was wandering loose in the English countryside. The old man trudged through the field, now and again putting his binoculars to his eyes and sweeping the landscape with them in a wide arc. He sighed. Nothing. He was disappointed. He had at least expected to have caught a glimpse of Auntie. Where had she gone? She was his own pet and he really hadn't expected her to stray far from the home she had known for so long. He had miscalculated badly with his idea of using the grey parrot as a lure. As for the smaller animals – well, it was like looking for a needle in a haystack. Only Skip was of any noticeable size, but Dobson realized the rabbit's speed could have taken him a great distance by now.

He tried to think of a way in which he could set himself on the right track. What would be a domesticated animal's first reaction on being released into the wild? To seek shelter, he decided, and then, after that, to search for food. And where would it look for food? Well, all the animals were more or less vegetarian in their diet, so what clues did that give him? Only that none of them would need to look far for the necessary items to keep themselves alive. Maybe, then, they hadn't yet strayed too far? Dobson was a little heartened by his reasoning. The one unpredictable creature was Spider. His personality demanded more than just the basic necessities for survival. He was intelligent and playful. He craved attention. He was also extremely agile and acrobatic and full of energy. There were few places which his boundless curiosity might not lead him to explore. And fewer still which would be beyond his capabilities to climb or enter.

Dobson passed within a metre of Pebble who was resting, head and legs withdrawn safely into his shell, in a clump of hogweed. The man's eyes were directed at the foreground and not around his feet. He trod a path through the tall dead grasses and brought himself into the wooded area. His field-glasses raked the tree tops. Only the woodland birds were to be seen. A blackberry or two on the wood floor meant nothing to Dobson and so he missed another clue.

Rather hopelessly he started to call, 'Auntie! Auntie!' His voice sounded forlornly through the tunnel of greenery. 'Spider! Where are you? Come on, Spider!' Only a woodpecker answered, laughing mockingly at his endeavours.

Dobson had been quite right about Skip. The rabbit

had already travelled a long way and always towards the windmill which, on its hillock, dominated the horizon. But, although he had run across one field and then another, the landmark never seemed to get any closer. He had outdistanced all the other animals. Eventually he found himself in a cornfield. The warm musty smell of the wheat, golden and ripe in the early September sun, persuaded Skip to pause. He nibbled tentatively at the plump ears of wheat, found them to his liking and roamed from row to row amongst the stiff rustling stalks. He forgot his loneliness for a while. He was tired and presently he lay down and fell asleep.

He was wakened by a tremendous roar of machinery. He leapt up in panic and dashed about, first this way and then another, trying to escape the terrible din. But, if anything, it appeared to come closer. Skip burrowed blindly deeper and deeper into the thickly clustered yellow stalks, desperate to hide; bury himself away. Quite unknowingly he was doing the worst thing possible. The wheat was being cut and harvested and the gigantic harvester with its massive rotating blades was clearing a wide swathe around the edge of the field. Skip cowered with a quaking heart in the very centre of the crop. He didn't know which way to turn. The earth shook all around him as the combine harvester drove relentlessly on.

Gradually the area of stubble widened and by contrast the uncut wheat shrank steadily to an ever smaller square. Now Skip knew the monster was closer. It was as if he could feel its harsh metal breath ruffling the very fur on his body. Frantic with fear he could keep still no longer. Then he saw a dart of movement.

Another rabbit, a wild one, plunged towards him through the diminishing ranks of wheat-stalks. It came face to face with Skip, its eyes wide with horror. It stared at him dumbly for just a moment, then dashed on past. Skip fled in the wild animal's wake almost without thinking, instinctively following the white blur of its tail. The wild rabbit hurtled pell-mell through the remainder of the standing crop and straight out into the open, jumping the bunched stubble and racing almost into the ravenous jaws of the mighty farm machine. The animal veered only at the last moment, saving itself by a fraction. Close on its tail, Skip saw the harvester with its accompanying tractor and wagon and he leapt high, turning his body in mid-air and, as he landed again on the vibrating soil, raced back towards the heart of the wheatfield.

The wild animal had reached the hedgerow bordering the field. Now it turned, expecting to see the strange brown rabbit behind. But it saw Skip going now in quite the opposite direction.

'No, no!' the rabbit called to Skip. 'This way! This way!'

The ruthless pounding of the machine drowned him out. But now Skip himself found the small patch of wheat no longer a safe haven and turned again. The machine roared past on its circuitous course and Skip bolted again into the open. His eyes glimpsed the grey body of the other rabbit under the hedge bottom and he ran towards it.

'Quickly,' called the rabbit, 'into the next field.'

Skip obeyed blindly. The two animals scrambled through the hedgerow into a meadow dotted with grazing sheep. Skip pulled up short. He had never seen these fleecy creatures before.

'It's all right,' said his new companion. 'We're not in danger here. Sheep won't bother us.'

Skip couldn't manage a reply. His heart was racing. His breath came in short gasps. The other rabbit waited for him to calm down, Then it said, 'Where did you come from? I've never seen a rabbit quite of your colouring before.'

Skip related as much as he could but the other animal merely gaped. Skip guessed it didn't understand what he was talking about.

'Where do *you* live?' he asked the wild rabbit.

The other mumbled something about a warren nearby which was just as unintelligible to the pet rabbit.

'Do you have a name?' Skip asked.

'A name?' repeated the rabbit. 'Of course I have a name. I call myself Fleet because I *am* very fast. And what about you?'

'I'm fast too,' Skip confided.

'No, no. Your *name*.'

'I'm Skip.' He began to groom himself, washing his paws and rubbing his face and ears.

'Are you going to live round here?' asked Fleet.

Skip paused for thought. 'Er – no,' he answered. 'I'm heading for the windmill.'

'Oh, is that to be your home then?'

'I – er – I'm not exactly sure,' Skip confessed. 'I just have to get there.'

'Why?' Fleet was puzzled.

45

'That's where I meet my friends,' Skip replied.

'Oh.' Fleet seemed to accept this explanation. 'Is it far?'

'Yes, it's far,' Skip answered, suddenly feeling very important. 'Don't you know the windmill?'

'Never come across it,' Fleet remarked. 'And I know most places around here. You must be very adventurous, you and your friends. All the rabbits I know stick to their own area.'

Skip was flattered. Then he said, 'They're not rabbits.'

'Not – rabbits?'

'Oh, no. My friends aren't rabbits.'

'What are they then, foxes?' Fleet asked jokingly.

Skip told him what they were. Fleet stared at him without a word. It was obvious he had never heard of such creatures. Then his expression changed. He seemed to lose interest and began nibbling at the herbage.

After a while he looked up and, seeing Skip still there, said, 'Oh well, I mustn't keep you from your friends.'

'You're not,' said Skip. 'I must be well ahead of them by now.'

'I have to get back to the warren,' said Fleet awkwardly. It was apparent he found something very strange about the brown rabbit. 'Good luck on your journey.' And he loped away.

Skip wanted to call him back; to tell him not to go. But somehow he felt Fleet wasn't comfortable with him and so pretty soon, apart from the sheep, he was alone again.

*

Pie and Thrifty had crossed the second field. Both of them were quite weary but each felt vulnerable on the ground. Pie wanted to climb into a bush. But the hamster's instinct was to get underground.

'Let's look for a hole,' she suggested. 'It'd be safer.'

'Well, if we must. . . .'

'We both need to rest.'

'I'm thirsty,' said the rat. 'I must drink first.'

'Where can you drink?'

'There's water somewhere about. I can scent it.' Pie's snout and whiskers twitched busily.

'Well, you must have a very powerful nose,' said Thrifty. 'I can't smell it.'

'Yes, yes, it's—' Pie scurried about searching for the right direction, 'it's, it's here somewhere. *I'll* find it.' He sat up on his hind paws, balancing himself with his long bald tail laid flat along the ground. His front paws tucked against his chest, he snuffled the air vigorously. Abruptly, he dropped back on all fours. 'This way!' he cried and ran off.

Thrifty had difficulty keeping up. Her store of food did weigh her down. But she scuttled after Pie gamely enough. It seemed to her a long while before the rat showed any signs of slowing up. She wondered if they would ever reach Pie's target. But at last, when Thrifty felt she really couldn't have run much farther without completely exhausting herself, she saw Pie stop ahead of her and begin to look around. He had stopped by a barbed-wire fence on the edge of yet another field.

'Have you – have you found it?' Thrifty gasped as she came up with him.

'Well, I – I thought I had,' Pie answered her

47

uncertainly. 'The scent is so strong, yet I can't see water anywhere. Can you smell it now?'

'Yes, but I can't see it either.'

Pie was perplexed. He looked all around in frustration. 'It must be here, it must be here,' he muttered continually. On the other side of the barbed wire was a long rectangular trough made of zinc. 'I'm going to investigate,' he told the hamster. 'You stay here out of sight.' He began to climb up one of the fence posts. The barbed wire presented no problem to either of these small creatures. He sat on top of the fence post and uttered squeaks of excitement. 'I knew it!' he cried. 'Thrifty, it's in there!'

The hamster peered up at him. 'What, in that thing?' she called back.

'Yes, it's a sort of giant water bowl. It must be a really colossal animal that needs all this water. Come and look.'

Thrifty shuddered. The last thing she wanted was to risk going anywhere near such an animal. 'No, no,' she answered hurriedly. 'I'm not thirsty at all. You have your drink and then let's get under cover before this giant beast comes back!'

Pie was amused. 'Don't be silly,' he said. 'D'you think I'd be perched up here in full view if the owner of this water bowl was anywhere in sight? There's nothing in this field, Thrifty. Whatever the animal is, it's not here now.'

But the little hamster wouldn't be persuaded. So, in the end, Pie clambered on to the edge of the trough which, fortunately for him, was very full, making it easy for him to reach the water. He drank gratefully. Thrifty was glad when he returned to the ground.

'Well, I'm satisfied,' he told her. 'Now, have you found a hole?'

'I haven't looked for one,' Thrifty confessed, 'but I'll do so now.'

'We'll look together,' Pie offered.

But, try as they did, there were no inviting bolt-holes, no tunnels and not even a convenient depression in the ground to be found in that field.

'Now what do we do?' Thrifty demanded. 'We came all this way for your precious water. There were holes a-plenty in the other spot.'

Pie had a knowing look. 'I think I may have just the answer for you,' he said. 'Come with me.' He led the weary hamster back to the water trough. 'Look,' he said. 'D'you see? This great water bowl doesn't rest level. There's a very nice gap underneath it at one end. Just room for you and me to sneak in. We'd be good and secure in there, don't you think?'

Thrifty didn't know what to think. But reluctantly she had to admit there were no other possibilities just then and she simply couldn't have gone on any further. 'All right,' she said. 'You lead.'

Pie scrambled into the darkness under the trough. There was plenty of room for both of them. Thrifty followed. They were well hidden but the ground was moist and dank where water had been spilt by drinking animals.

'It's better than nothing,' Pie pronounced cheerfully in reply to the hamster's grumbles. 'We won't have to put up with it for very long.'

Thrifty was reminded of their ultimate destination. 'How far do you think it is now to the windmill?' she asked.

Pie hadn't a clue but he wasn't going to admit it. 'We've come a good way already,' he remarked. 'We must just keep on looking out for it.'

Before falling asleep, Thrifty emptied her pouches of the berries she had collected and she and Pie munched them in silence. Then they huddled together for warmth in their damp resting place and both were soon oblivious of any discomfort.

Later on they were rudely awakened. The cattle who normally occupied the field had returned from their milking. Their great teeth and long rough tongues tore at the pasture. Soon some of them had rasped a path close to the water trough. Thrifty opened her eyes, hearing the heavy tread of hooves. The noise echoed in the little animals' hollow of mud and metal.

'Pie!' she squeaked. 'Pie! The gigantic animal's come to drink!'

The piebald rat awoke to semi-consciousness. 'What? What was that?'

'The monster—' Thrifty began; then her voice was drowned by the steady slurp of water as half-a-dozen bovine heads were lowered to the water trough. Some of the water slopped to the ground as the great slow beasts stirred the trough's contents and, as it trickled into the hidey-hole, Pie and Thrifty's bodies were threatened with saturation.

'Quickly, out of here!' Pie ordered, and the two tiny animals scampered out and into the late sun-shine, weaving their way through the forest of legs and hooves, the owners of which, docile and slow witted, scarcely even noticed their passing.

——— 7 ———

A Reconciliation

Spider stopped running only when he reached the shelter of a hedgerow. He sat down where he could lean his back against a stout hazel stem. One of the fingers with which he clutched the bananas was still sore from Auntie's angry peck. Spider put the bananas on the ground next to him and sucked his throbbing finger thoughtfully. Moments later Auntie fluttered down beside him.

'You and your beak,' Spider complained. 'You don't realize what a vicious weapon you've got there.'

'I'm sorry, Spider,' Auntie said contritely. 'It all happened so quickly. I – I didn't think.'

'All right,' said the monkey. 'We'll forget it. But I hope you won't attack me again?'

'Oh no, we're friends, aren't we?'

'I sometimes wonder,' said Spider ruefully. He pulled a banana from the bunch and started to peel it. Auntie's eyes fixed on him eagerly. She put her head on one side and shuffled her grey feet. Spider knew she was watching him. He made her wait a while.

'I suppose you want some?' he enquired at length, grinning at her with his yellow teeth.

'POP! POP!' Auntie uncorked excitedly.

Spider held out a piece with finger and thumb. The parrot took it very gingerly in her beak, using excessive caution to avoid nipping the monkey again. Spider grinned as Auntie blinked in delight at the ripe flavour of the banana. Together they worked their way through three of the stolen fruit.

'Ah,' Spider breathed when they had finished, 'now I'm sleepy. But I don't want to drop behind. Skip runs fast. He may be ahead of us.'

'Tell me,' urged Auntie, 'what's so important about the windmill? Why do you want to be the first there?'

'Because I want to be the first to claim it,' Spider answered mysteriously. 'You see, when I was in my cage in the shop I used to see the windmill on its high point, beckoning to me day after day like an old friend. It has a special significance for me and I have to go back – er – go there. And now that all of us are free, we can all go.'

'I don't understand,' Auntie returned. 'Why does it have this secret meaning for you? As the only bird amongst us I could fly straight there if I wanted to. I could soon find out what there is to know and bring word back to you.'

'No!' Spider denied the idea vehemently. 'I have to go myself.'

'Then let's go quickly and get it over with, so that I can get back home.'

Spider looked at the parrot in astonishment. 'Home?' he echoed. 'D'you mean the shop?'

'Of course I mean the shop. That's my home, isn't

it? Not this expanse of grass, trees and so on as far as the eye can see.'

'But you were confined there; chained up most of the time,' Spider argued. 'What sort of a life was that?'

'The only sort of life I've ever known,' Auntie replied promptly.

Spider had no answer. His only recourse was to continue on the way.

Skip had lingered in the field with the sheep. For one thing he half hoped that Fleet would make a re-appearance. Also there was an abundance of clover in the field and Skip found the sweet leaves and flowers very much to his liking. The noise of the combine harvester and the tractor eventually ceased and the air was peaceful.

After a while Skip was tempted to return to the cornfield in case Fleet might have decided to do the same. He tunnelled through the hedge and was amazed at the altered appearance of the crop in which he had hidden. The wheat was harvested; only the stubble and bare earth remained. Here and there a few ears of wheat were scattered on the ground where the jolting wagon had spilt them. Skip looked around for signs of Fleet. The wild rabbit was not to be seen anywhere. However, two older, more familiar friends were running along one side of the field, stopping every so often to gather the wheat kernels. Pie was crouching and eating them with relish. Thrifty was eating one for every three she stored. Skip loped over joyfully. The animals greeted each other.

'I'm so pleased to see you,' the brown rabbit said earnestly. 'I hate being on my own.'

They exchanged stories of their adventures. Pie embellished the episode with the cattle but Skip was unimpressed. Nothing could compare with the roar and power of the metal monster he had run from.

'We'll all travel together now, shall we?' he asked with bated breath. After his disappointments with Pebble and Spider and then Fleet he wondered if anyone wanted his companionship. But Thrifty reassured him.

'Of course we will,' she said, 'won't we, Pie?'

'The more the merrier,' answered the rat. 'I wonder where that monkey's got to? I can't help feeling there's something devious about him.'

'I think you're right,' Skip affirmed at once. 'I saw him – and Auntie. Spider didn't want my company at all. And I saw Pebble early on as well. *He* said he was far too slow for me. So I'm really glad we've met up.'

'So am I,' said Thrifty sweetly. 'There's comfort in company, isn't there?'

'Talking of comfort,' said Pie, 'we need to find somewhere snug before nightfall.'

'Yes, and dry,' Thrifty emphasized, 'not like the last place. Have you seen anywhere, Skip?'

'Can't say I have,' replied the rabbit. 'I know there are some rabbit burrows hereabouts but – well, maybe they wouldn't welcome us.'

'They'd welcome you, surely?' Thrifty suggested.

'I don't know,' said Skip awkwardly. 'Anyway, we'd better find something to accommodate all of us.'

'Which way do we go now, Pie?' asked the hamster. 'I've rather lost direction.'

54

'Into the next field, of course,' said Pie. 'That's how we always go – until we get there.'

'I've already been in it,' Skip told them, feeling a little superior. 'Watch out for the sheep. They're harmless but big.'

'You've been there?' Pie queried. 'Then why are you here? You're going backwards.'

'Oh no, not really. I was just looking for – for someone to talk to.'

Dusk was gathering by the time they had filed through the scattered sheep. And now they faced a problem. So far their travels had taken them on a gentle but steady downhill course. The sheep field was at the end of the drop and, at its bottom, ran a little brook. The animals had to cross this in order to get to the next field in which there was a group of outhouses belonging to the neighbouring farm. Pie saw the scope for sheltering amongst these buildings.

'Perfect,' he said. 'Perfect. Just what we were looking for.'

'But how are we to get there?' demanded Thrifty, looking at the brook which was about a metre and a half in width.

'Easy,' the rat answered her confidently. 'We'll paddle over.'

'Swim? Across that?' To the little hamster the brook was a considerable challenge. 'I've never swum in my life.'

'We have to be adaptable,' Pie pointed out, 'if we're to get to the end of our journey. After all, travelling across countryside in broad daylight is not exactly a commonplace thing for a hamster and a rat, is it? Our normal inclination is nocturnal. But we couldn't see the windmill if we went by night. So we're already doing things we wouldn't have expected to do.'

'Well, *I'm* not going to swim it,' declared Skip. 'I shall leap across. Perhaps you could jump it too, Thrifty?'

'Don't be absurd!' she snapped. 'Have I got your great bounding hind legs? If you can't be more helpful than that. . . .'

'I'll be more helpful,' said Pie. 'I'm not much bigger than you and if I can swim it, then so can you.'

'Oh, you're different, Pie. You take everything in your stride. I'm not like you. I just *know* I'd drown. I'll stay here.'

'Nonsense. I'll show you. Then you do as I do.' Pie ran to the water's edge, took a few sips and then immersed himself in the brook, kicking out strongly for the opposite bank. In a few moments he was pulling himself clear of the water. His black-and-white fur clung to his body in a lump making him look half his usual size. 'You see?' he called across. 'It's quite simple, Thrifty.'

Thrifty didn't like the look of him. He didn't at all resemble the animal who had been her neighbour for so long in the pet shop. She began to back away in alarm, afraid of how her own appearance might be altered.

'Thrifty, come back! Skip, talk to her,' Pie cried urgently. 'Don't let her go.'

The rabbit managed to soothe the little animal and calm her fears. But then, just as she was ready to enter the water, he did a foolish thing. Thinking to urge her on, he leapt over the brook, landing next to the streaming rat and leaving Thrifty deserted on the far bank.

'Oh, Skip!' squealed Pie in exasperation. 'Now look what you've done.'

The rabbit's great jump had startled Thrifty and she had half slipped and half stumbled into the brook. The wheat kernels she had stuffed into her food pouches made her top-heavy in the water and her head was submerged. Instead of at once striking out with all four legs for the shore she panicked and, despite the slow current, Thrifty began to be carried downstream. Skip loped along the bank, keeping abreast of her and bewailing his stupidity, but seemingly without the faintest idea of how to help her.

'Do something. Pull her out!' cried Pie in vexation. 'She's lost otherwise.'

Fortunately Thrifty came to rest just then against a piece of fallen branch that had lodged midstream. Instinctively she scrambled up and along it, then sat shivering and quaking with cold and shock.

'I'm sorry, Thrifty,' Skip called to her miserably. 'I didn't mean—'

'Don't waste time with words, you great lummox,' Pie scolded him. 'We've got to get her over here. Quickly now!' He ran down to the edge of the water to see what was their best remedy. One end of the branch trailed underwater and across to the bank on their side of the stream. Pie grasped it with his strong molars and tugged. The strength of his jaws was quite unequal to the task. 'You try!' he ordered Skip.

Skip's larger teeth and more powerful build managed to pull the end of the branch out of the water and on to the bank. Now Thrifty had a little bridge to run over.

'Come on then,' Pie called to her. 'Be careful you don't slip off!'

The hamster crept forward. The branch was wet and slimy but her claws gripped it firmly and she edged slowly along. As she neared the bank she felt the branch waver. She didn't hesitate. She jumped and landed with a little plop in the mud at Skip's feet. Her golden fur, already plastered to her body, was now coated with a film of ooze. She shook herself energetically. It was growing dark.

'Let's find some cover and dry out,' she said. 'My teeth are chattering.'

Pie took the lead. They headed for the nearest of the buildings. A peculiarly robust and pungent odour came from it. They heard the grunting of pigs.

'We'll steer clear of this one,' Pie decided. 'There's something inside.'

The next construction was more promising. It was an open-sided barn, half-full with bales of hay. The animals pushed themselves in amongst these, uttering little cries of satisfaction and relief. They were easily able to conceal themselves and the closely-packed hay served both to dry and warm them. Thrifty pushed at her cheek pouches and out came the wheat husks.

'Those things were nearly the death of you,' Pie reminded her.

'Don't you complain,' she said. 'Our bodies may

be wringing wet but at least I've kept our supper dry.'

As night began to close in Joel Dobson gave up his fruitless search. His animals were about to spend their second night out in the open and he trudged disconsolately back to the shop, shaking his head. He closed the door behind him and, seeing the solitary guinea pig moving restlessly in her cage, he felt a sense of kinship with the little creature. He opened her cage and picked her up, stroking her affection-ately. He could feel Candyfloss quivering in his fingers.

'Yes, you're not used to being handled, are you?' Dobson murmured ruefully. He thought about the other animals. 'Poor little things: none of you are. I should have done more of it. Or if I didn't I should have let someone else. 'Then perhaps,' he spoke to Candyfloss, 'we wouldn't be in this position now. Well, I'll make it up to you. You're not going to stay down here all by yourself. You're coming upstairs with me from now on. I'll fix something up for you. We'll console each other.'

Later that evening the old man received an unexpected visitor. It was Eric. He appeared at the shop door looking shamefaced and sheepish. Dobson let him in.

'Well!' he exclaimed. 'You've got a nerve, I must say, coming back here. After all the—'

'I know. I know all that,' the lad broke in hastily. 'I know what I did was wrong and stupid. Don't you think I've regretted it? I've come to make amends and offer my help if – if you'll take it.'

'Help? What sort of help?'

Eric threw his arms wide. 'To look for the animals,' he said.

'I've been looking all day,' Dobson growled. 'I didn't see so much as a whisker.'

'Well, I did,' Eric said dramatically.

'Where?'

'In the town.'

'The – town?' Dobson muttered. It was the one place he hadn't thought of looking.

'Yes,' said Eric. And he went on to tell the old man of Spider's and Auntie's tricks.

Dobson couldn't restrain a chuckle. 'Well, I'll be blowed,' he said. 'And you didn't try to catch them then?'

Eric explained that it would have been impossible at that time. 'But I think we will,' he added. 'After all, a monkey and a parrot can hardly go unnoticed, can they? We're bound to get word of them.'

Dobson nodded. 'I think you're right,' he said. 'And they're the ones I'm most concerned about. Auntie's mine, you know that. And Spider was supposed to be in my care. As for the others, I fear they'll be beyond our reach by now.'

'Is it a truce then?' Eric murmured.

'Very well. I know I didn't do all I should,' the old man said honestly. 'You dropped hints enough. But, by the way,' he suddenly reminded himself, 'I've got one of the animals back already.'

'That's marvellous! Which one?'

'The guinea pig. I don't think she liked the Great Outdoors.'

Eric looked downcast. 'They're all defenceless

really, aren't they?' he muttered. 'I realize it now. That's why I came over.'

Dobson looked at him with some sympathy. 'All right then, Eric,' he said. 'Let's put the past behind us. From now on, we'll manage together.'

—8—

Rain

While Pie and Thrifty were drying themselves in the barn with Skip, Spider and Auntie were also looking for shelter. They had reached the stream which Spider cleared at a bound but the barbed-wire fence had presented him with a difficulty. It was in his nature to climb and swing and jump, yet none of these faculties were of any use here. The lowest strand of the wire ran so close to the ground that only an animal used to burrowing or squeezing through narrow gaps could have got under it. It didn't occur to Spider to attempt to wriggle underneath so he sent Auntie to see if there was another way into the field.

In the gloom of the evening it was not easy, even for the bird from her unique position aloft, to find another route. All she could see was barbed wire stretching in either direction into the distance. She brought the news to Spider.

'Oh well, it's time to choose our roost anyway,' he said. 'Here's our spot.' He indicated an ash tree that had been allowed to grow up tall in the hedgerow. And, without further ado, he shinned up the trunk. Auntie wasn't so keen to spend the entire night in this isolated tree. She was drawn to human habitations. She thrived on the nearness of human noises and chatter and she decided to wait until Spider was asleep and then fly close to a building. She perched near the monkey and watched him closely, reminding herself all the time of her preference by running through her repertoire of impressions.

'HELLO AUNTIE. HAVE A GRAPE. WINDMILL PET SHOP. D'YOU WANT A NUT? RING! RING! GOOD OLD GIRL!' And so she went on, interspersing her recital with squawks and lavatory flushings. Spider listened to the tirade with growing irritation until he could stand it no more. Auntie was defeating her own object because the last thing the monkey was able to do was sleep.

'Look,' he said, 'if this is your idea of a game I don't appreciate it. Whatever are you trying to do – advertise where we are for the master's benefit?'

Auntie choked back the next utterance. The monkey was clever. He'd half guessed her thoughts. Spider settled himself more comfortably in the crook of a branch. Auntie held her peace. But all the time her beady eyes watched him and watched him. . . .

When she was quite sure that Spider was asleep, she sidled along the branch to its far end so that the clatter of her wings on take-off would be less detectable. Then she flew into the darkness, her only guide the beam of light from a farmhouse window. Her efforts at subterfuge, however, failed. Spider stirred as his sleeping bough rocked. He opened his eyes and looked around. He called the parrot periodically, but he guessed she had deserted him.

'I don't need *her*,' he muttered to himself and went back to sleep.

During the night a wind got up and blew rainclouds across the area. The first drops fell on Spider as he slept. He wrinkled his nose but didn't waken. Eventually the leaves began to drip steadily as the rain intensified. Spider's fur became damp, then wet. He awoke and shook himself. The rain had now become a downpour. Spider realized his shelter was inadequate. He scrambled down the ash trunk, gibbering with exasperation. All along the hedgerow the vegetation was sodden, offering him no shelter. He had to look elsewhere. He ran back to the barbed-wire fence and bounded along its side, searching for an opening. All the while the rain dashed down, soaking his fur. Spider began to feel very miserable. Then, on one of the barbs he saw a strand of brown fur. He bent to examine it. At once he recognized it as belonging to Skip the rabbit. And he had, indeed, come to the point where the three smaller animals had passed under the wire. Spider looked at the ground and he looked at the wire with the piece of fur. He realized Skip had scrambled underneath here. Now he understood how to get into that field. He lowered himself, grimacing with distaste, on to his belly. The ground was cold. Quickly he wriggled and pulled himself through and, once through, the dark shapes of the outbuildings met his gaze. Here was shelter!

Just as the others had done, he skirted the pig enclosure and came next to the barn. But in Spider's case the open barn in a rainstorm didn't seem to be the ideal place to settle. So he went farther. He came to a long low enclosed building. He ran alongside it. He couldn't see a way in. He bounded up on to the shed roof to explore its possibilities. There was no entrance there and despite the lightness of his hands and feet, he aroused the occupants of the building. A chorus of clucking and squawking like the noise of a thousand different Aunties broke out inside. The battery hens were alarmed and they, in turn, alarmed Spider. He leapt off the roof and galloped away, back in the direction of the barn – anywhere to escape that awful cacophony. He raced into the barn and buried his head in the hay to shut out the noise. The rain drove in and spattered his poor drenched body. Spider tunnelled his way into the comforting musty smell of the dry dead grass.

'Hello, Spider,' said Skip. 'Where's Auntie?'

The monkey started but quickly recovered from his surprise. 'I knew you'd be here,' he fibbed. 'You left a trail.'

'Thrifty and Pie are here too. They're drying out,' Skip explained.

'Just why I'm here,' Spider returned. 'What a night!'

'Did you fall in the stream?' piped up Thrifty.

'Stream?' Spider echoed. 'No, no, I didn't fall in anything.'

'He's been out in the rain,' Skip told the hamster.

Now Pie joined in. 'So we're all together again. Except for Auntie and Candyfloss. I wonder where they are?'

'Auntie's somewhere nearby,' said Spider. 'She was with me until nightfall. As for Candyfloss, she didn't like the open air, did she? I expect she went back. And you've forgotten Pebble.'

The animals fell silent, thinking their own thoughts. Skip missed Candyfloss and wasn't entirely sure whether he wouldn't rather be back with her, even if she was in the shop. The others were thinking about where they would end up the next day. Spider's chief thought was of food. He had used up his bananas and he had to find a fresh supply of food at first light. Pie and Thrifty were wondering how far it was to the windmill and what other obstacles they would have to face.

'How do you find your food?' Spider suddenly asked, his mind full of the subject.

'Pick it up as we go along,' Pie spoke for the others. 'It's easy, especially when you're in Thrifty's company. She hoards everything for later.'

'You don't need much, I suppose, you small ones,' Spider mused. 'But you're not so small, Skip. Thrifty couldn't collect enough for you?'

'Oh no. I find my own. I never realized there was so much variety. The world's full of food,' Skip remarked.

'I haven't found it quite so simple,' Spider admitted. 'Perhaps I'd better stick with you for a while, Skip?' he added jokingly.

'Oh, I see, now I'm of use,' Skip returned. 'When *I* wanted *your* company you sent me away.'

Spider grinned. 'No harm meant, you know. We're all friends together, aren't we?'

'When it suits you,' the rabbit mumbled.

The rain continued to splash down outside. No one thought much about Pebble. They all guessed he was

66

far, far behind them. But Pebble was thinking about them.

Pebble was easily able to look after himself. Dandelion and clover were abundant and he could survive on those plants alone for a while. He managed to find some young shoots to his liking too. His shell was his shelter. He had no need for extra cover. But, like all the animals, he was used to company. Now, because of his ponderous plodding pace, he was condemned to an enforced solitude. He thought about his old companions all the time and how they used to talk together. Pebble liked to talk. So he was always on the look-out for someone else to take the place of the friends he had lost. When the rain began Pebble was only just nearing the end of the first field. He didn't mind rain. In fact he rather enjoyed the novel feel of moisture on his leathery old skin. But when it became very heavy Pebble decided enough was enough. He withdrew into his shell. Occasionally he shifted his position slightly and the intriguing motion of what otherwise appeared to be no more than a lump of rock drew a fascinated audience.

A couple of toads who lived amongst the damper parts of the nearby vegetation sat and contemplated the unusual sight. Wet weather always persuaded them out of hiding and they became far more animated then than they ever were when it was dry. They had been dining on the slugs and earthworms which also had been revelling in the rain. The toads had paused from their banquet to squat and study Pebble's shell. Neither spoke for a while. But when the tortoise did hear voices he slowly began to peep out.

'What do you think it is, Speckle?'

'Looks like a sort of brick to me, Wart.'

Pebble's horny head emerged a little.

'Oh, it's never a brick!' cried Wart. 'It moves!'

'Of course I move,' Pebble said in his dry, slow voice. He had established that he was quite safe as the onlookers were smaller than he was.

The toads jumped at the unaccustomed sound. Pebble's legs protruded from his shell and he lurched forward a couple of steps.

'He walks!' exclaimed Speckle.

'That's just what I *must* do,' Pebble murmured to himself, 'if I'm ever to get where I'm going. Walk and walk and keep on walking.'

'Where are you heading?' the toads chimed in together.

'The windmill,' replied Pebble. 'I don't know how far it is.'

'Oh, the windmill,' remarked Wart. 'He's going to the windmill, Speckle.' (Neither of them had the faintest idea where it was.)

'Hadn't you better hurry a little?' Speckle enquired as they watched the tortoise's gravely slow gait.

'I *am* hurrying,' came the answer. 'Can't you see?'

The toads thought this a tremendous joke. 'Very droll,' Wart observed. 'You have a nice sense of humour. I like that.'

'Very necessary,' Speckle agreed.

But Pebble didn't feel at all humorous. However, he wasn't resentful. 'You've obviously never come across a tortoise before,' he surmised. 'But I know what you are. Frogs. There were some in the shop once.'

'Frogs! Of course we're not frogs!' Wart retorted irritably. 'Nothing *like* them; foolish, nervy creatures.'

'Toads,' said Speckle. 'Toads. That's what we are. D'you understand?' He raised his voice as if dealing with a creature with a hearing disability.

'As you say. It makes no difference,' said Pebble nonchalantly and he passed them by. 'What rain! We shall be afloat soon.'

The toads watched him a little longer. His extraordinarily laboured progress was a marvel to them.

'What a strange animal,' said Speckle.

'He is. We don't want to lose sight of him,' replied Wart. 'He's rather interesting, like a giant snail with legs.'

'Not likely to lose sight of him, are we?' Speckle remarked dryly. 'We could clear up every worm and slug in this field and still keep him in view.'

Wart laughed a croaky laugh. 'He's very determined, though. I bet he'll get to the windmill he has in mind.'

The toads went back to their feeding. They were indeed quite impressed, the two of them, by this animal who resembled a brick. They planned to keep a check on him.

In the barn it was dry and warm. For Skip, Thrifty and Pie there was plentiful food within easy reach of their shelter. Although they remained curious about the windmill, each of them began to wonder in their own minds why they needed to travel any farther than they had already. For them, the power of the windmill, which had featured so strongly in their outlook from the shop, was beginning to wane.

Auntie rested on the farmhouse roof, her head tucked under her wing. Eventually the rain drove her under the thatched eaves. All she could find to clasp was a trellis nailed against the wall which was clothed in clematis. It was a precarious perch and she waited impatiently for the human inhabitants to stir.

——9——

Farm Visitors

The rain had woken Joel Dobson during the night. His immediate thought was of the animals. His mind dismissed any fear for the well-being of the rabbit, the rat and the hamster, and also the tortoise. He knew they could cope. His worries were centred on the monkey and the parrot – creatures from exotic climes who could only survive away from their natural habitats if given sufficient extra warmth and shelter. To date the September temperatures had posed no threat. Rain was another matter. It wasn't warm tropical rain they were exposed to; it was cold relentless English rain, thoroughly chilling and penetrating. Dobson couldn't get back to sleep. He got up. The little guinea pig, which he now kept with him above the shop, was scratching about in her hutch.

'Well, Candyfloss, you're better off where you are,' the old man mumbled. He switched on the light and bent to look at her. 'What a nice cosy little nest you've made for yourself, haven't you?' He reached inside and picked up the warm, soft, yielding animal. Candyfloss was becoming used to his caresses. He

71

stroked her smooth fur and she lay quietly in the crook of his arm. 'Got to get your friends back,' the man told her, 'before they suffer.'

He was impatient for the daylight. He and Eric were to meet at seven o'clock to co-ordinate their search. That gave Dobson three hours before he opened the shop. After ten, Eric would continue alone. The man put Candyfloss back in her hutch and went into his kitchen to make a pot of tea. There were a lot of hours to kill before he could do anything really positive.

At the first sound of human voices Auntie became alert. She cocked her head on one side and uttered a few exploratory noises beneath her breath. 'WIND-MILL PET SHOP. BRRR. BRRR. HELLO. WINDMILL PET SHOP.' Then, with the utmost satisfaction at her own abilities, she let out a quite deafening screech as if to announce her presence.

The family were having their usual early breakfast. Auntie's screech interrupted their conversation. Initially they thought the cry had come from one of their ganders, but the next instant they found themselves an audience to the parrot's stock of impressions which included a lifelike imitation of Dobson taking payment from a customer. 'THANK YOU MADAM. THAT'LL BE . . . .' (She hadn't heard an identical sum of money quoted sufficiently often to have quite mastered the last bit.) 'THANK YOU MADAM. BRRR. BRRR. WINDMILL PET SHOP. HAVE A NUT.' At the end of her recital she even managed a fair representation of Spider's gibbering. But this meant

72

nothing to the people indoors. They thought they had a madman outside.

Faces peered out of windows but couldn't see anything to explain the tirade. Auntie was well hidden amongst the greenery of the climbing plant. There was a slight pause. The faces disappeared from the windows to exchange mystified glances with one another. There were exclamations of astonishment. Stimulated by this, Auntie began again. 'HAVE A GRAPE PET SHOP. HELLO AUNTIE WINDMILL. POP! POP!' She was so excited that the words and sounds tumbled out anyhow. Corks were drawn from at least an entire case of claret and the family also heard, without any possible doubt, two separate flushings of a lavatory.

In one mass movement they rushed to the door, several hands trying at once to undo the same locks and handles in their collective eagerness to get outside. They burst from the house, startling Auntie and sending her squawking to the roof top.

'It's a parrot! It's a parrot!' they cried, pointing her out to each other.

Auntie gazed down and ruffled her feathers. The early daylight picked out her grey plumage. 'HELLO AUNTIE,' she murmured to herself consolingly. The farmer, his wife and two sons exploded into laughter.

'Hello Auntie!' they called back in unison.

'Where's it come from, Dad?' asked one of the boys.

'How on earth should I know?' he responded. 'But we'll have to try and catch it. It must have escaped.'

Auntie showed no sign of wanting to leave her high

position. She was beginning to enjoy the attention and, now that the skies had cleared of cloud, she could see for miles. In the near distance, dominating the surrounding scene as always, stood the windmill. She intended to visit it, before Spider got there, to see what all the fuss was about. But there was plenty of time for that. She hadn't finished with the entertainment yet. 'POP! POP!' More bottles were opened. Then the telephone began to ring again. 'BRRR. BRRR. RING. RING. WINDMILL PET SHOP. HELLO.'

'So that's it!' exclaimed the farmer. 'It's from the pet shop! Might have guessed it. Right, we must make sure we get it back there.'

But it wasn't as simple as that. Auntie had no intention of returning to the pet shop until she herself should decide it was time. The family soon realized she wasn't going to come down just yet.

'Perhaps if we go back inside, she might be tempted closer?' suggested the boys' mother.

'Good idea,' agreed her husband. 'We'll put some titbits out and see what happens.'

'What sort of titbits, Dad?'

'Oh, I don't know – what do parrots eat? Fruit, I should think. We can chop some apple up. Something like that.'

'I'll do it, I'll do it,' cried the younger boy, very excited by the whole event, and he ran back indoors.

The other boy followed. 'You finish your breakfast first,' their mother cautioned them.

Later a dish of apple and orange pieces was placed by the farmhouse porch. The boys waited breathlessly for the parrot to appear. Auntie had indeed ventured from the roof top back to the trellis, a little disappointed by the sudden silence. However, it was quite a time before she noticed the offering of fruit.

'HAVE A GRAPE, AUNTIE,' she reminded herself and edged closer, trying to make sure first there were no competitors for the food supply. Her beady eyes looked all around her. There didn't seem to be anything between her and the fruit. She was unaware that, inside the house, four pairs of eyes were glued to her every movement. So Auntie hopped to the ground and sidled towards the bowl. The family decided to let her eat for a while without interruption. They were amused and impressed by her delicate manners. The way in which she held a segment of orange in one claw whilst she took ladylike nibbles from it with her grey tongue and beak entranced them. But eventually the farmer thought it was time to make a move to secure her.

Carefully he opened the farmhouse door. Auntie looked up from her meal but didn't see any immediate threat. She selected a slice of apple. The farmer crept forward. His two excited sons jostled in the rear and it was the boys' impatience that saved Auntie. She saw their impulsive movements out of the corner of her eye. With the apple still in her beak she flew upwards, back to the safety of the roof.

'Now look what you've done!' The farmer rounded on the boys. 'I nearly had the bird! Now we'll never reach it!'

His sons looked crestfallen. Auntie swallowed the apple and squawked triumphantly. 'HELLO AUNTIE. D'YOU WANT A BIT OF BISCUIT?' she called.

'All's not lost,' said the boys' mother. 'We know the parrot's name now.'

'Do we?' mumbled the farmer uncertainly.

'Of course we do. She calls herself "Auntie". Haven't you heard her repeating it?'

'Good, good. Well done,' said her husband. 'We'll ring the pet shop later. At least we can give them a lead.'

But Auntie wasn't long on the roof. She decided to fly away from what seemed a risky area, human companionship notwithstanding. She had to see the windmill before any more permanent relationship with people was taken up again.

At seven o'clock Joel Dobson and young Eric met at the pet shop.

'Well, have you any ideas?' the old man asked. He told Eric where he had searched the previous day.

'I saw Spider and Auntie in the town,' said the youth, scratching at his ginger head. 'I don't think you were looking in the right place, Mr Dobson. We ought to concentrate on the outskirts of Wandle.'

'Humph! Have you had any breakfast?' the shop owner grunted.

'Yes, thanks. I boiled myself some eggs.'

'Better get going then. You lead the way to where you saw them and we'll start from there. I'm really worried, Eric, about that rain.'

The young man noticed the definite note of concern in Dobson's voice and was impressed.

About an hour after they had left the shop the telephone rang. It was the farmer hoping to give news of Auntie's sighting. So the best clue for them as to how to proceed was lost.

*

In the barn where the animals were sheltering a shadowy figure flitted about in the dawn light. A fox, on its way home after a night's hunting and roaming, had picked up the pets' scent with its keen nose. It trotted to their hidey hole in the hay but it couldn't see them, so deeply embedded in it as they were. The fox wasn't hungry which was just as well for the animals because, had it been, it might have dug around more. As it was it didn't bother but went padding away on its springy legs – but only a little way away, so that it could keep its eye on things, just in case. . . .

Spider awoke first and his first sensation was one of cold. It was a feeling to which he was entirely unaccustomed after the artificial heat of the shop. He hadn't been exposed before to the damp raw air of an English dawn after rain. He tried to push and pull himself deeper into the musty bales and immediately disturbed all his companions.

'Is – is it time to move?' Thrifty asked sleepily.

'It's nearly light,' Pie answered her. 'Are you quite dried out?'

'Quite dry, quite dry,' she assured him.

'Speak for yourself,' Spider affirmed. 'I'm famished. But – oh, it's so cold out there.'

'You'll soon warm up, once you get going. We'll run about a bit,' suggested the rat.

'We can always come back here later,' the hamster suggested. 'It's a marvellously cosy nesting place.'

'Yes,' said Skip. 'Why do we need to go any further except to find food? We couldn't find a better spot than this. It suits all of us.'

Spider forced himself into the open and shook

himself vigorously. Actually his fur was dry now but the air continued to make him shiver. His teeth began to chatter. He ran across the floor and leapt on to a pile of bales. Then he bounded from one pile to another and down to the floor in a flurry of activity. His blood raced through his veins, and his fingers and toes and ears began to tingle with warmth. He rejoined his friends, grinning happily.

'We must continue our journey to the windmill,' he told them authoritatively. 'Only if we get all the way there will you understand the greater comfort it offers.'

'You talk in riddles,' Pie grumbled.

'Don't you remember,' the monkey went on, 'how we used to wonder what it would be like to make the journey to the windmill and be able to look back at that tiny little world which was all that we knew? Well, we can do that! Can't you see, we're much closer now? Closer to those great spreading arms, opened wide to welcome us, to gather us into its embrace. How often before, in our little pens, did we yearn to be gathered up and embraced? We never got such comfort there.'

The smaller animals didn't understand much of what Spider was saying. But his enthusiasm communicated itself to them. The clever monkey was so persuasive. And they did remember the windmill beckoning to them from its hillock with its arms open: a symbol of something they lacked and towards which they had been drawn, almost without their realizing it.

'So you see,' Spider was saying, 'we have to go on if

we're ever to have that comfort.' He saw that the animals were ready to follow him.

They gathered themselves together, keen to press on. Now that the rain had ceased, the brightening sky promised fairer weather. They ran out of the barn, each animal's fur liberally sprinkled with fragments of straw. The fox saw them go. Its eyes widened at the sight of the strange human-like creature which bounded along at the front. Its chief interest, however, was reserved for the plump brown rabbit. It slunk after them with a quiet unhurried pace.

The animals neared the farmhouse where Auntie had recently surprised the inhabitants. Pie, Thrifty and Skip were wary of the big strange building but Spider sensed there were people inside and this attracted him to it with its prospect of food. He ran on ahead and at once came across the dish of fruit, still more than half full, which the household had provided to tempt the parrot. Spider congratulated himself and plunged in one paw.

'I don't want to go as close as that,' Thrifty said, seeing the monkey on his haunches right by the porch.

'Let him go,' said Pie. 'He can look after himself and join us later. Let's skirt this place, shall we, Skip?'

'I agree,' said the rabbit. There was a smell of dead animals – meat, game, whatever it was – coming from the house that frightened him.

Pie branched off at an angle, giving the farmhouse a wide berth. He, Thrifty and Skip entered the vegetable garden. All the plants were drenched. The aroma of cabbage, lettuce and all sorts of green plants filled Skip's head. He loitered. Pie and Thrifty threaded their way along the neat rows of growth. A more robust smell that came from the compost heap interested the rat. He loved pungent odours and he adored strong flavours. Potato peelings, maize husks and rotting vegetable stalks littered the rubbish pile in the corner of the garden. Pie made a beeline for it and attacked the litter with gusto. More from habit than anything else, Thrifty followed him.

Skip nibbled a fresh lettuce leaf, absorbed in his enjoyment. Slowly, carefully, the fox approached on silent feet, always keeping hidden, always concentrating on the necessary stealth. Gradually it came closer, then paused behind a screen of stakes over which vigorous growths of runner beans were swarming. Here the fox was perfectly hidden, yet was close enough to wait for the perfect moment to pounce.

Skip munched on. Pie was tackling a crust of stale bread; Thrifty had been drawn from his side by the scent of overripe strawberries, the remains of a late crop, and she had found a strawberry bed at the edge of the garden. Spider, having polished off the parrot's leavings, was unsatisfied. He looked around and up at the house, watching for signs of life. The farmer was preparing to start work, his wife about to take the boys to school. The fox waited on, patience personified. It meant to kill the rabbit and take it home underground quickly, before the daylight was too revealing.

Thrifty ate a strawberry, a large one. Then she gathered two or three more and pushed them into her pouches. They were large fruit and she looked

forward to a feast later. Spider sauntered along the
side of the farmhouse towards the vegetable patch.
He stopped to examine a pair of drainage pipes lying
by a trench, ready for use. Men would soon be
arriving to work on the new system the farmer needed
for his badly drained fields. The monkey, ever
curious, peered inside the pipes. He could tell they
were too narrow to allow further exploration and so
he turned his attention elsewhere. He saw Thrifty
amongst the strawberry plants and hastened to join
her.

'These are good,' she told him. 'Try them.'

Spider needed no further encouragement. He
began to eat greedily, stuffing them into his mouth.
The sweet soft fruit were delicious. He found more,
clusters of them, dark red and overripe. He ate them
all. He was ecstatic. He had never eaten strawberries
before and now he worked the row thoroughly,
parting the leaves and plucking handfuls of fruit. In
between mouthfuls he gibbered his enjoyment.
Thrifty ate another one. Soon the two were joined by
Pie. The rat had suspected he was missing out on
something.

All at once several things happened. The farmhouse door opened and the whole family spilled out,
talking noisily. Skip bolted from the disturbance
instinctively, leaving a half-eaten lettuce behind him.
The fox, just as instinctively, raced after him,
unwilling to pass up a chance of a kill. Spider, Thrifty
and Pie saw Skip running towards them across the
garden with the fox in hot pursuit. The farmer cried
out at the sight of the fox and swore profusely. He had
reason to dislike foxes as a menace to his livestock.

81

The boys pointed and shouted at the monkey; it was as if a small zoo had taken up residence in their neighbourhood and they'd never been so excited. But Spider managed to keep his head. He could see Skip was in deadly danger and that Pie and Thrifty and even himself were threatened by the predator fox. He remembered the pipes.

'Follow me, all of you. No time to lose!' He raced back the way he had come. Skip, Pie and Thrifty ran for their lives. The fox had lost a little ground because it had slowed up, startled by the human cries. But now it was running full tilt again, as much to escape from danger itself as anything else. It kept on the same track, in the wake of the pets. Spider reached the pipes first and leapt on top. They were far too narrow to be a hiding place for him.

'In here, in here,' he shrieked.

The rat and the hamster dived easily into the dark interior, their clawed feet pattering on the plastic base. Skip was close behind. There was just room for him to scramble inside away from the fox's jaws. But he was a far stouter animal than his friends and, in the impulse of flight, he had run in too fast. The impetus of his rush now wedged him so tightly to the pipe's walls that he was well and truly stuck. Ignoring Spider, the fox ran on past, cheated of its prey and with the farmer chasing it and bellowing angrily.

Pie and Thrifty scuttled on unthinkingly, still frightened by the turn of events. They reached the end of the pipe and raced on out of it and over the ground. But Skip the rabbit was trapped, held fast in the pipe's circumference. He shivered in fear, unaware that two pairs of kind young hands were coming to collect him.

——10——

Auntie at Odds

Auntie was distant from the scene of Skip's recapture by this time. She flew across country, directly on course for the windmill. From the ground, no one who wasn't out specifically bird watching would have noticed anything unusual about her. Her colour and size could have been mistaken for that of a wood pigeon. In fact in flight, apart from her scarlet tail feathers, Auntie made a rather drab figure.

She flew over fields where cattle grazed and paddocks where horses stood lazily by fences, gazing at nothing particular with their soft friendly eyes. Then the windmill loomed up ahead of her, black and still, its sails so massive they looked too heavy to turn. Auntie began to search the surroundings for a clue. She expected to spy something significant that would give her the key to the mystery of the wooden building. After a while she fluttered to a halt, perching on a cherry branch. She felt puzzled. She was on the edge of a little orchard, now overgrown and unkempt with weeds. The untended trees had produced little fruit and what sparse crop there was had mostly been eaten already. In front of her was the windmill, motionless and empty. There was a door at its base and windows in the sides at various levels. It had long ago ceased to be a working mill and had been converted into a dwelling. But now it was unoccupied and forlorn. Around the exterior were a number of dilapidated wooden pens and hutches which meant nothing to the parrot.

From this high point at the top of the hillock Auntie had a wonderful view of the rolling country-side. She looked back over the terrain she had crossed. Then she looked all around at the immediate area. She could see nothing that enlightened her. She thought of Spider and the other animals and wondered just what they expected to find here. The monkey especially had seemed determined that this should be their goal. For the life of her Auntie couldn't think why. She stared and sought in every direction.

'There's nothing here,' she muttered to herself, 'unless I don't know what I'm looking for. I'm only a bird and Spider's so much more clever.'

She didn't move away at once. There were a few small black cherries still clinging to her tree. She hopped amongst the branches, pecking them off one by one. In the orchard a blackbird and a mistle thrush were devouring other remnants of the crop from the unpruned trees. Auntie pondered whether to approach them. She was uncertain of her reception, remembering the little darting martins who had chased her in the town. But then, she thought, they might – just might – know the secret of the place. She put discretion behind her and fluttered towards

85

them. The smaller birds, busy with their gleaning didn't, at first, notice her.

'Do you know this place?' Auntie squawked nervously. 'I – I mean,' she added, 'do you live here?'

The blackbird swallowed a piece of cherry and regarded her. The thrush ignored her completely, transferring its attention to some windfalls.

'Who are you?' the blackbird fluted. 'And why are you asking?'

Auntie considered how to respond. 'I'm a parrot,' she said awkwardly. 'And I'm puzzled.'

'A puzzled parrot,' the blackbird seemed to mock. 'Whatever that may be.'

'I – I just want to know about the windmill,' said Auntie.

'The windmill? I don't live there.'

'No, but do you know anything about it?'

'I know as much as you do, at least,' the blackbird answered cryptically, 'that it is a windmill.'

'Is it – is it a special place?'

'I don't know what you're on about,' said the blackbird.

The thrush was listening, its head cocked on one side. Presently it sang out, 'It's deserted.'

'Yes, I can see that,' returned Auntie, a bit more confidently. 'Has it always been?'

'Long as I can remember,' came the reply. 'But I was only fledged in the spring.'

Auntie was emboldened. 'Is there anything special around here?' she persisted. 'You know – something secret?'

'The orchard's a secret to all but a few,' the blackbird piped up. 'How did you know about it?'

Auntie was flummoxed. 'I didn't,' she said defensively. 'Well, not until I came here.'

'Where did *you* come from then, puzzled parrot?'

'Back there,' she answered. She looked behind her, over the green fields, to the town. The huddle of buildings was quite visible on the horizon where they appeared to be struggling up the hill. The last building at the top of the hill was the pet shop but Auntie didn't recognize it in the distance.

'Are there more of you coming?' asked the thrush, thinking of the supply of cherries.

Auntie misunderstood. 'Oh yes,' she said. 'That's just it. They're all coming here and – well, that's why I wanted to know about things.' She thought she had struck a chord. These birds knew about their coming. So there must be something here!

The thrush and blackbird glanced at each other. They accepted one another as well as other neighbourhood birds as competitors in the orchard. But the idea of a horde of strangers arriving to raid the trees didn't please them at all. And, just like Auntie, neither the thrush nor the blackbird realized they were talking completely at cross-purposes.

'I think,' said the blackbird with a glint in his eye, 'you'd better tell your friends that we shall prepare ourselves for their arrival.'

Auntie, mistakenly, was pleased and she looked it. The pets were to be welcomed! Somehow their journey to this destination had been expected. Her look of pleasure, however, didn't meet with a like response. The two smaller birds glared at her darkly.

'I'll tell them,' Auntie squawked gleefully in reply. 'I'll tell them to expect a reception.'

The blackbird fluted angrily, 'There'll be a reception all right.' He turned to the thrush. 'Won't there?'

The thrush piped, 'Indeed there will.'

Auntie felt she had achieved something. She couldn't wait to get back to Spider and tell him the good news. She was so excited she pulled half-a-dozen explosive corks so unexpectedly that the thrush and blackbird flapped away, thoroughly alarmed.

'Next time you see me I'll have company,' the parrot screeched after them.

The smaller birds resettled themselves. 'So will we,' the blackbird shrilled menacingly. But Auntie didn't hear. She was in the air, heading back for the tree in which she thought Spider would still be sleeping. 'THANK YOU MADAM. THAT'LL BE . . . .' she cackled as an accompaniment to her flight.

Of course Spider was no longer in the ash tree. With the threat of the fox removed he ran, with Pie and Thrifty, from the altogether kindlier threat of grasping hands. The farmer's sons removed Skip gently from the drainage pipe. It was obvious to the whole family that the collection of animals was connected with the appearance of the amusing grey parrot a short while before. The rabbit was put in a safe place before the boys were driven to school, and the farmer agreed with his wife that she should telephone the Windmill Pet Shop again later in the morning.

Joel Dobson returned to the shop, once again, empty handed, just before ten o'clock. He had left Eric to continue this disheartening search for a glimpse of the pets in and around the town. The shopkeeper was worried and irritable. Mechanically he turned the sign on the shop door to OPEN. All at once the telephone rang. Dobson stumped over to the instrument, pulling at his ragged moustache.

'Hello? Windmill Pet Shop.'

The voice at the other end sounded relieved. 'At last! I've been trying you for hours. I've some news for you.'

'News? Really? Who's speaking please?'

'Mrs Stickells from Stream Lane Farm. Have you lost a parrot and – and—'

'Yes, yes,' Dobson broke in excitedly. 'I have. Have you found her?'

'Well, not exactly. We've *seen* her. She was at the farm but we couldn't catch her. She was just too quick for us.'

Dobson's heart sank. 'Have you seen anything else?' he asked disappointedly. 'A monkey, for instance?'

'Yes, we have. There were lots of them here – I mean, lots of animals,' Mrs Stickells corrected herself, 'and we *have* managed to recapture one of them.'

Dobson's spirits rose again. 'The monkey?' he cried breathlessly.

'No, I'm afraid not. It's a rabbit.'

'Oh, only a rabbit?'

'Yes, a brown one.'

'That's mine all right.'

'He got stuck in a pipe, but he's not hurt.'

'A pipe? How odd. Well – look, thank you, Mrs

Stickells. I've been out searching for them all. I'll come and collect the rabbit from you. Can you keep him till lunchtime? I've only just opened the shop. You can? That's very kind. Well, goodbye. And thanks again.' He replaced the receiver. Only Skip. But at least the Stickells had seen Auntie and Spider. That gave him a lead.

'Oh, Eric!' he exclaimed to the absent boy, 'You're in quite the wrong place.' They had arranged between them that Eric would ring the shop at midday or sooner if he had anything to report.

The door clicked. The first customer of the day entered.

Auntie didn't have to fly all the way to the ash tree. Spider was instantly recognizable as quite different from any other animal in the countryside and she soon saw him bounding along the perimeter of a field watched by a curious mare and her foal. Pie and Thrifty were not so easily visible but they were keeping up with the monkey pretty well since, every so often, he would stop and wait for a spell. Auntie swooped down.

'There you are!' she called. 'Guess where I've been.'

'No idea,' said Spider uninterestedly.

'To the windmill!'

'What?' snapped the monkey. 'You've been there already?' He sounded annoyed.

'Yes. I wanted to see what all the fuss was about. So I – flew there.'

'You had no right to,' Spider told her. He was

furious with the parrot for stealing a march on him. 'You shouldn't have done that.'

'Why ever not?'

'The windmill's my domain. I should have been there before any of you. Or at any rate we should have gone together,' he muttered as Pie and Thrifty came up. 'Er – say no more about it now,' he whispered hastily.

Auntie looked askance. What was Spider planning? A surprise for the others? She exchanged perfunctory greetings with the rat and hamster as Spider told her about Skip.

'Oh,' said Auntie, 'we're a dwindling band, aren't we? We should get to the windmill as soon as possible and get it over with.'

'Get what over with?' the others chorused.

'Um – well,' answered Auntie carefully, 'I mean our journey. Then we can go back.'

There was silence. Eventually Spider repeated quietly, 'Go back?'

'Yes, of course; to the shop. What else would we do?'

'So that's still what you have in mind?' Spider murmured. 'Well, I don't think we're all in agreement.'

'*I'm* not going back,' Pie declared at once. 'Otherwise why did we ever get out in the first place?'

'You didn't get out; you were put out,' Thrifty, who had mixed feelings, reminded him.

'Yes, but – well, we're here now, aren't we? How could we go back to those cramped cages?'

'I wasn't in a cage,' Auntie remarked superciliously.

'Ah – that's it,' Spider said craftily. 'It doesn't matter to you then, does it? Well, we won't detain you. You tell me you've done your trip. You may as well set off home again straight away. Come on, Pie; Thrifty.' The monkey ran on as if he had quite washed his hands of the parrot. Pie followed. Thrifty lingered.

'I'm not sure what we're all up to any longer,' she confided. 'But I suppose I'd better go along.' She scurried away.

Auntie watched them go, half in astonishment and half in dismay. She hadn't even had a chance to tell them what she had seen at the windmill. She perched uncertainly on a fence post. Should she go back to the shop or follow the thing through with the others? She thought of the birds' reception committee in the orchard and wavered. She wanted to go home but, on the other hand, she didn't want to miss anything interesting. She raised a foot and gave her head a scratch, unable to make up her mind.

Spider raced on ahead of the others. In his anger he had forgotten to pause. However, despite the fact that he was seething, he really longed to know what Auntie had found at the windmill. He began to wonder if he had been too hasty. He slowed down to a lope and eventually stopped altogether. He stood up on his hind legs and looked back. He couldn't see Auntie who was still sitting on the fence post. The monkey gibbered with frustration.

Auntie didn't hear him but she evidently sensed something because she all at once made up her mind. She decided to fly after Spider. She was rather surprised to find him waiting for her.

'I thought you'd come,' Spider muttered, 'so I waited.'

Auntie squawked with pleasure. 'Well, now I'm here, do you want to know what I found out?' she asked.

Spider couldn't disguise his eagerness. 'Yes, yes,' he said impatiently.

'They know we're coming,' Auntie announced importantly.

Spider was taken aback. '*They* – know?' he muttered. He looked mystified.

'Yes. And they're preparing themselves for our arrival.'

'Preparing themselves?' Spider echoed. 'What do you mean? And who's "them"?'

'Well, the birds, of course,' said Auntie. 'In the orchard.'

'Orchard! Birds! What on earth are you talking about? I want to know about the windmill.'

'The windmill itself? Oh, it's closed up,' Auntie replied. 'And quite empty as far as I could tell.'

Spider's face suddenly changed. He looked stunned. 'Empty?' he whispered. 'But – it can't be.' He seemed to forget that Auntie was there, and immersed himself in his own thoughts.

Pie ran up. 'Hello – I thought you'd abandoned us,' he said to the parrot.

'It was me who was being abandoned,' she answered caustically.

Pie noticed Spider's faraway look. 'What's up with him?' he asked.

Auntie knew the monkey didn't want her to

93

mention the windmill. She could only think of one answer. 'Perhaps he's missing Skip,' she said unconvincingly.

——11——

Spider at School

When Eric telephoned Joel Dobson at twelve o'clock the old man gave him the news and told him to return to the shop at lunchtime. Then, together, they went to Spring Lane Farm to collect Skip.

'He doesn't seem any the worse for wear,' Dobson remarked when they had put the rabbit safely into the car. 'Just a bit grubby, that's all.'

Mrs Stickells had given them all the clues she could as to which way the other animals and Auntie had gone and Eric thought he would stay around there and see if he could trace them.

'Good idea,' Dobson agreed. 'They may not have gone far yet. You can ring me as soon as you discover anything. I'd better be getting back.'

Skip was soon sharing accommodation with his old companion again but now the hutch was much more roomy. Candyfloss was overwhelmed by the rabbit's return. She could hardly believe it. Skip was equally pleased to see her. They nuzzled each other affectionately and ran about the hutch, tumbling one another over in their mutual excitement.

When they had quietened down Skip said, 'We

seem to be in a different place. It feels like an age since I was in the shop.'

'We are in a different place,' Candyfloss told him. 'The master brought me up here as soon as he found me again. And, do you know, Skip, he seems to have changed.'

'Has he? In what way?'

'He's much more caring and friendly than before. He really seems to enjoy my company now, which has been so nice because I *have* been lonely, you know, since I've been the only one here.'

'Well, that's all over now,' Skip said comfortingly. 'And I must say I've no regrets. It's a strange sort of life out there and very frightening at times.'

'Is it? Do tell me about it. You see, I didn't go anywhere at all.'

Skip was a little amused by her plaintive remark. He launched into a tale of his adventures, adding many embellishments to the incident of the harvester. Candyfloss was absolutely enthralled. Afterwards she said, 'I wonder what's happened to the others. I do hope they're safe.'

Spider came abruptly out of his reverie as the other three stared at him. There was a Junior School nearby and he had caught the sound of children's voices – dozens of them – raised in play. His inquisitive nature came to the fore, overriding all other considerations. Without so much as a glance at Auntie, Pie and Thrifty, Spider headed off towards the excited, boisterous noise, determined to be a part of it. It was in his nature to be playful. He forgot all about the windmill, which was in quite another direction; he only had ears for the children's joyful chatter. Once again he was allowing his main objective to be sidetracked by curiosity.

Auntie knew he was going the wrong way and when the other animals started to follow him, as usual, she called them back. Spider was running so fast he soon disappeared from view.

'No good going after him; he's got some new idea in his head,' said the parrot.

'How do you know?' asked Thrifty.

'Because the windmill's *this* way,' Auntie replied. And she flew a little way forward to demonstrate.

'Then what—'

'Don't ask,' Pie interrupted. 'Spider's behaving strangely. Let him do as he decides.'

Spider made a beeline for the source of the noise. He saw the happy, laughing children in the playground and redoubled his efforts. Just outside the school railings he halted and sat on his haunches. He grasped the railings in his long fingers and gibbered with excitement. The children were so absorbed in their play they didn't see him at first. But Spider was a past master at drawing attention to himself. He shinned up an iron post and sat on its flat top. Then, hanging by one arm, he swung out and snatched a rubber ball which was rolling along the ground. Two boys, who were in hot pursuit of the ball, shrieked in astonishment. They were the very same boys who had seen Spider at their father's farm earlier that morning.

'Look! Look!' cried Peter Stickells, the elder boy. 'Hey! Come back!' Spider made off with the ball, clutched in his long fingers.

'It's the same monkey,' said his brother, David, incredulously. 'He must be following us.'

Spider had run to a corner of the playground where he was examining the pink rubber ball, his face wearing his favourite bemused expression. He turned the ball over and over in his hands; smelt it, bit it, then dropped it in disgust at the taste. The ball bounced and, fascinated, Spider grabbed it again and juggled with it. The mysterious object appeared to have a life of its own. Spider climbed into the fork of an ornamental cherry tree that grew in the playground, intent on seeing what else the ball could do. By now he had caused quite a commotion and most of the children were converging on the tree.

Spider chattered excitedly and suddenly hurled the ball at the approaching group. A score of hands reached out to grab it.

'He wants to play! He wants to play!' the children chanted shrilly.

Spider became more and more excited. He saw the ball pass from hand to hand. Sometimes it dropped and bounced, then it was seized again and thrown or rolled amongst the clamouring group. The monkey couldn't sit still. He watched the children and watched the ball and gibbered impatiently. He awaited his chance. All at once he leapt from the tree and landed right on top of the ball in the midst of the mêlée. This time he smothered the ball to his chest, then raced across the width of the playground and bounded on to the low porch at the school entrance. The children pelted after him, Peter and David at their head with a fine sense of superiority because their ball and (they felt) their discovery, the monkey, was claiming the attention of the entire playground.

The teacher on duty had finally observed the cause of the furore. She called the children to order, quietening the screams and shrieks. Then she stepped towards the porch.

'Does anyone know anything about this monkey?' she cried, a little excited herself.

David piped up. 'He was at our house at breakfast, Miss. He's come from a zoo!'

His elder brother corrected him. 'Not a zoo, silly; a pet shop.'

'Whose is the ball?'

'Ours!' they chimed together.

'Do you know anything else about the pet shop?'

'I can't remember the name of it but my father tried to tell them about their monkey. And there's a parrot as well,' Peter finished importantly.

The teacher looked about her, as if expecting to see this creature somewhere in evidence too. 'Where did—' she began, but her voice was drowned by a great whoop from the children. Spider was climbing up the slate roof over the school hall. The teacher followed the children's gaze. She craned her neck and saw the monkey reach the apex of the roof where he sat down, nursing the ball.

'I'm afraid you've lost your ball, Peter,' she told the boy. 'The animal seems to like it.'

'Bet he'll throw it down in a minute, Miss,' one of the other children said. 'He's playing with us.'

Spider was actually waiting to be chased. He knew he was in a game and he wanted the fun to continue. When none of the young people in the playground made any move to follow him he tried to entice them into action. He stood on the roof and gesticulated, baring his yellow teeth and gibbering at them encouragingly. When this didn't have any effect the monkey sat down again and began to contemplate his toes. He fingered each of them in turn as if they were strange objects he had never seen before.

'Hadn't we better rescue him, Miss Potter?' asked a little girl.

'I don't quite see how we can do that,' the teacher answered uncertainly. 'But perhaps Mr Gilson can think of something.'

Spider was becoming bored. The children's clamour had died down and he wondered if he had been forgotten. He stood up again and suddenly, in a fit of pique, he slung the ball at the crowd gathered beneath. As before, the children jostled each other for possession. The winner was a big loutish boy who elbowed all the others out of the way. Then, taking aim, the child flung the ball back at the monkey. It struck Spider smartly on his back, nearly knocking him off balance.

'You stupid boy!' shouted Miss Potter. 'Whatever do you think you're doing? Come here at once!'

The oafish boy grinned, as if proud of what he had done.

'It's not even your ball!' David Stickells cried angrily.

The teacher grabbed the offender and hustled him inside. Spider, winded and rather frightened by the blow from the ball, teetered along the roof top and then, with a flying leap, launched himself into space. He landed nimbly enough on the roof of the neigh-bouring building which abutted the walls of the

100

school. This building was the home of Mr Gilson, the school caretaker. Meanwhile the ball trickled down the slates and lodged in a gutter.

In Miss Potter's temporary absence the children now surged over to the wall dividing the playground from Mr Gilson's garden. They shaded their eyes to look up at the athletic Spider who had stunned them all by such a leap.

Spider, none the worse after all, preened himself, pulling aside tufts of hair on his arms and legs to look for foreign bodies. He was the centre of attention again as the children's concerned and wondering voices flooded over him. Miss Potter reappeared on the scene.

'He jumped, Miss. He jumped!' the children shrieked. 'Look where he is now. He jumped right off the roof on to next door!'

'All right, all right,' said the teacher. 'Playtime's over. Calm down now, all of you. The monkey seems all right. Now, indoors with you and no dawdling. Go to your classes. I'm going to have a word with Mr Gilson.'

The children filed back into their classrooms, still talking animatedly. Gilson had heard the crash on his roof and had come out to his garden to investigate.

'Well, blow me!' he exclaimed. 'I don't believe it. A monkey! Now where in heaven's name—'

Miss Potter entered the garden at that moment and gave him a hasty explanation. 'Two of the boys know a bit about it,' she said. 'The animal's escaped from a pet shop. Can you get a ladder or something – try and grab him? We'll have to ring round all the pet shops in the district later and try and find out where he belongs. I don't know if there are many in the area.'

'I know where the nearest one is,' said Gilson. 'Be best to try there first, I suppose.'

'Yes. Well, I'll leave you to it. I'll have to get back to my class or they'll be running riot. I'll speak to you later.'

Gilson went to his garage and took out his long ladder. Spider watched the proceedings with interest. He watched the man carry the ladder to the wall of the house and prop it against the gutter. Then he watched the man climb the ladder, step by step. He saw his face appear at close quarters. The man spoke gently, calling to him. Spider hesitated. Was there a titbit on offer? He came a little closer as the man continued to talk to him. Closer and closer. . . . Then the man did a silly thing. He tried to grab Spider by the nearest leg. The monkey scuttled away, screaming at him. Gilson cursed. Spider climbed up on top of the chimney, still gibbering angrily. What did they take him for? Gilson pulled himself up on to the roof, testing it carefully for strength. He realized there was no chance of his actually stepping on to it. But Spider didn't know that. He naturally thought the man was coming to capture him. He turned on the chimney, preparing to make another leap. But he missed his footing and suddenly he slipped backwards and down. Down, down he slithered, all the way through the filthy black chimney until, with a great bump, he landed on the brick hearth and lay quite still.

—12—

A Blaze

Pebble had reached the patch of woodland at the edge of the first field and had become confused. The gloominess under the trees didn't appeal to him at all. He liked light and warmth. Moreover, he wasn't sure which was the best way out of the wood. He waddled about for a time, tasting a variety of leaves as he went. Most of them were not to his liking.

At dusk he looked for a secluded spot and withdrew into his shell. The two toads, Wart and Speckle, had kept the tortoise within reach and came in search of him. They preferred to be active during the nocturnal hours. It was Speckle who stumbled across the immobile shell.

'Here he is, Wart,' he croaked. 'Here's our rock.'

Pebble heard the voice but didn't stir. He was halfway to slumber and hoped he would be left alone. It was a vain hope, of course.

'Hiding again,' Wart remarked. 'But I must say this is the best form of defence I've ever seen.'

'Yes,' Speckle agreed. 'A fox or a badger would have difficulty in tackling him.'

'Perhaps they would sort of – prise him open?'

103

suggested Wart. 'They're so determined, some of them.'

'I think their teeth would shatter if they tried that,' mused Speckle. He paused. Then he said, 'He doesn't appear to want to come out. What a pity. I had hoped for more of a reaction than this.'

Pebble regretted the toads' intrusion into his rest period. Not because he wished to remain alone – he didn't – but because he would much have preferred their comradeship in the daylight hours when he felt more lively. But he thought he shouldn't risk appearing rude. He poked his head out of his shell.

'Why do you always want to talk when I want to sleep?' he asked with wry humour.

'Why do you always want to sleep when . . .' Wart began jocularly.

'All right,' said Pebble. 'I know. It depends how you look at it, doesn't it?'

'You're still making for the windmill?' Speckle enquired.

'Yes, I – actually, that's where you fellows can help me,' Pebble said earnestly. 'I've got a bit lost in here – I can't see far ahead of myself; trees everywhere. Can you point me in the right direction?'

'Right direction for what?'

'The windmill, of course.'

'Oh, yes. I see,' said Speckle. 'What – now?'

'No, no, not now. Too dark to see anything,' Pebble said patiently. 'But when it's light again, if you don't mind.'

The toads looked at each other uncertainly. They didn't really know what the windmill was, but they didn't want to let on so they played for time.

'The trouble is,' said Wart, 'we're not very active during the day. It's a risky time for us.'

'Dogs, cats and humans,' Speckle explained.

'And traffic,' added Wart.

Pebble wasn't put off. 'Not in the wood surely?' he said shrewdly.

'No, not in the wood. But – round about.'

'All I want is a guideline,' Pebble explained. 'Just tell me the path to take and I'll do the rest. I won't put you in danger.'

'The path to the next field?' Wart conjectured.

'Well, yes, I suppose so.'

'Simple. Good as done,' replied the toad. 'We'll leave you in peace. Come on, Speckle. Back at sunrise,' he called back over his shoulder.

'By the way,' said Speckle, 'what's your name?'

'Pebble,' said Pebble.

Pie and Thrifty were making good progress. Auntie made sure they kept the right course. She thought constantly about the planned reception in the orchard and how they would all eat the fruit together. She was dying to tell the small animals that she had already been to their destination and back again. But she remembered Spider's reaction on hearing the news and held her tongue.

All three of them wondered what Spider was up to. As the day wore on they were puzzled that he hadn't rejoined them.

'Perhaps he's lost himself,' said Thrifty.

'Not him,' said Pie. 'Too clever for that, he is. I think he's got into a scrape.'

Auntie recalled the greengrocer's stall. 'He enjoys

a prank,' she said, 'especially amongst humans. He just loves to entertain them.' She hadn't forgotten how he had upstaged her. 'Though there's one thing he can't do,' she said with satisfaction. 'He can't copy them like I can. THAT'S IT. THAT'S IT. HAVE A GRAPE,' she demonstrated.

Pie and Thrifty froze. They were silent: the human noises always bewildered them. Auntie misinterpreted this.

'Are you tired?' she asked. 'Do you want a rest?' The parrot's normal voice reassured them.

'What do you think, Pie?' asked the hamster.

'I think we shouldn't push our luck too far. That's what I think,' he answered. 'We've been running freely out in the daylight for a long while. Sooner or later we're going to come across *something* unfriendly.'

These problems didn't concern Auntie. 'What do you want to do then?' she asked.

'Look for a permanent nest.'

'Permanent? What do you mean, Pie?'

'We can't risk ourselves indefinitely,' he explained. 'We have to have a base.'

'Yes, I'm all in favour of that,' agreed Thrifty. She felt herself to be exposed in the vast expanses around them. 'But what sort of a base? And where would we find it?'

'We could find it anywhere on our way,' Pie replied. 'It could be something like the place where we all sheltered from the rain. That was ideal.'

'I don't think we'll find another one quite like that.'

'Maybe not, but we can look.'

Auntie had no idea what they were talking about.

106

Of course she knew what a nest was. And she knew it was built off the ground, usually in a tree. But she couldn't for the life of her think how Pie and Thrifty could set up home in a tree even if they could climb it in the first place. However, she tried to be helpful.

'There are plenty of trees near the windmill,' she squawked without thinking.

'Is that so?' remarked Pie. 'Well, that's nice to know.' His sarcasm was lost on Auntie. But Thrifty cast the parrot a keen glance.

'How do you know what's near the windmill?' she asked.

Auntie realized she had said more than she should. She got a bit flustered. 'Er – well, from the air,' she said awkwardly, 'I can see a lot more than you can.'

This explanation satisfied both the small animals, who had no reason to suspect her.

'Now then,' said Pie, 'let's not stand around in the open like this, making ourselves targets. We ought to get to cover.'

A clump of dock proved to be ideal. The rank thick-leaved plants shaded them. Auntie perched on a sapling while Thrifty ejected the rather squashed strawberries from her cheek pouches and she and Pie made short work of them.

They continued on their way in the late afternoon. The windmill was really quite close now. It loomed up ahead on a slight rise and whichever way they ran it was never out of their sight. Auntie paced herself to keep alongside them. She was feeling mounting excitement as they pressed ever closer. Pie was still keeping both eyes wide open for a likely nesting site.

107

A solitary cottage came into view in the near distance. It was small but it had a lot of land which was enclosed by the flimsiest of wire fences – just two strands threaded at intervals through slender stakes. At one end of the area was an enormous pile of rubbish, far bigger than the one in the farmer's garden. This rubbish consisted entirely of dead vegetation – stalks, plant prunings, leaves, dead flower heads, lawn cuttings and the like. It smelt rich and inviting, Pie thought. And he also noticed there was a considerable amount of warmth generated by the pile. As far as the rat was concerned, that permanent nest was found.

'Thrifty – look!' he squeaked triumphantly. 'What do you think of that?'

The hamster stood up on hind legs and sniffed long and laboriously. 'Seems safe enough,' she said. 'Yes, I think we could blend in there quite well.'

'Come on then. Let's explore.'

The two animals raced for the inviting pile, heedless of Auntie who endeavoured to rein them back.

'Wait, wait!' she called. 'What about the windmill?' Failing to halt them, she reluctantly flew after them, landing on the very top of the rubbish heap.

'You've still a field or two to travel,' she told them, 'before you get there.'

'Plenty of time for that,' Pie answered, burrowing into the pile and feeling its dank, pungent warmth. 'We've both shelter and food here, Thrifty!' he cried excitedly. 'We need go no further.'

'But the *windmill*,' Auntie begged them.

'Tomorrow will do for that,' the rat replied. 'Leave us be now, Auntie. Come back in the morning.'

Auntie was dismissed. She was as good as forgotten by the two small creatures. She felt miffed. 'After all my efforts,' she muttered. 'A lot of appreciation I get. I don't know why I bother.'

They were deaf to her complaints, their interests entirely absorbed.

'And where am I supposed to go?' the parrot screeched. 'I'm to be on my own, am I? Thanks for your concern.' She was angry and hurt. She uncorked some particularly lively sparkling wines to ease her frustration.

Thrifty, who was kindly, relented. 'We'll be all right here for the night,' she said, 'but it's no place for you. You must make yourself comfortable elsewhere – you know what's best for you. But I hope you won't go far because we'll need you in the morning.'

Auntie was mollified. 'All right, Thrifty. We've done pretty well, haven't we? We've come a long way.'

'Yes, and still no sign of Spider. We may have to go on without him.' The hamster disappeared into the stack of rotting vegetation.

Auntie left them. She swooped over the cottage, looking for signs of food. There was nothing suitable. She was tempted to return to the orchard where the blackbird and thrush had promised a special greeting on her arrival. But she decided it would be better to leave that until she and the others could arrive together. She found a crop of maize and, fluttering from one long stalk to another, she carefully pulled off beakfuls of the plumpest corn. She enjoyed the sweet

109

taste so much she ate more than was good for her and eventually she flew awkwardly to a roost in a hornbeam tree, feeling as if her body was twice as heavy as normal.

As evening approached, Pie and Thrifty dozed together in the warm core of the rubbish pile. A black cat from the cottage came out for its nocturnal prowl. Unhurriedly it paced the length of the fenced-in land which was its own personal territory. After a while its sensitive nose caught the smell of the rodent pair, asleep and blissfully unaware of its threatening presence. The cat slunk to the end of the garden, its eyes skinned for the slightest hint of movement. Fortunately for the two innocent sleepers, there was nothing save their lingering smell on the air as a clue that they were nearby. The cat searched industriously. It guessed the animals were still around and it meant to be close at hand when they should show themselves.

When daylight came again the animals were to face a new danger against which the threat of the cat faded almost to nothing. It was a still day and the retired owners of the cottage had decided it was the perfect day for a bonfire. It wasn't much after six o'clock when Mr Grice came out to the garden, his pipe firmly clenched between his teeth. He was carrying matches and a small can of paraffin. He had been looking forward to burning the rubbish: he enjoyed a good blaze and had only been waiting for the right conditions. Mrs Grice joined him soon afterwards.

Despite the recent rain, the bulk of the rubbish underneath the outer layers was well and truly dry.

Mr Grice laid his firelighter equipment down and fetched the lawn rake. He began to pull the damp garden cuttings away. Inside the pile Thrifty and Pie felt the vibrations with alarm. But they only burrowed deeper inside to escape detection. The rubbish was soon ready for lighting. Mr Grice poured a little paraffin here and there. Mrs Grice handed him the matches. The day was devoid of any breeze. It needed only one match to set the bonfire going. The paraffin caught with a whoosh and the dry leaves and twigs soon crackled and curled. At the sight of the flames the cat bid a hasty retreat.

It wasn't long before heat and smoke reached the interior of the rubbish pile. The two little animals were petrified; neither could speak. Soon the heat was intense. It was Pie who moved first. He felt his bald skinny tail singe. He fought his way out of the hole, deaf to the human voices which would otherwise have kept him hidden. Thrifty, panic-stricken, scrambled after him. In their terror they actually ran down one side of the smoking vegetation where the flames had been held at bay by the dampness.

'By golly, look at the rats!' Mr Grice shouted to his wife as the animals tried to escape. Mrs Grice shrieked. Her husband snatched up the lawn rake and poked at the animals, trying to pinion the black-and-white rat. But Pie was far too quick. He scuttled for cover and was soon lost from sight. Thrifty, however, was not so quick. As usual her cheek pouches were charged with titbits which weighed her down. The rake jabbed at her and caught her by one leg. She thrashed and squirmed but couldn't free herself.

Mrs Grice came to look. 'For heaven's sake, Dick,' she scolded, 'that's not a rat. It's a hamster and somebody's pet! I hope you haven't damaged it.'

13

Sold

Only three of the pets were still free and mobile. Auntie flew up and down, looking for signs of her friends while steering well clear of the roaring bonfire. She feared the worst. Pie, however, was cowering under some logs; shocked, scorched and singed and only a matter of metres from the Grices' cat who was biding his time till the fire was out. As for Pebble, he trundled on impassively, across another field, unhampered and unnoticed by all save the two toads.

Thrifty wasn't badly hurt. She'd been trapped by the flat of the rake's prongs and was soon freed by Mrs Grice, who carried her indoors to examine her. There were no bones broken; only a gash on one leg. Mrs Grice bathed the tiny limb, put some ointment on it, then bandaged it delicately and finally stowed Thrifty in a cardboard box amongst some soft rags and shreds of newspaper. She had no idea what to do next. The Grices' cottage was a good distance from the nearest neighbour's and she couldn't think where the hamster could have come from. She made up her mind it was a child's pet and so must have travelled from afar since the nearest neighbour was a widow who lived alone. She could think of nothing other than to put a notice in the pet shop window in Wandle saying the little creature had been found, hoping to attract the eye of the owner's parents. In the meantime she must find out how to look after it herself.

Spider lay on the cold hearth, stunned and bruised. He was filthy: soot-black and festooned with cobwebs. Before the monkey had recovered his wits, Gilson the school caretaker came into the room and ran to the fireplace. He scooped the monkey into his arms. Now Spider began to struggle and bite. It was obvious to the man that the monkey's fall had caused him no serious harm.

'You little devil!' he cried as Spider bit his hand. It was a painful bite and Gilson made sure after that that the monkey's head was firmly held. The caretaker had no love of animals and already an unscrupulous idea had come into his mind regarding the monkey. Gilson's brother-in-law was a street photographer down on the coast. He wondered just how interested the man might be in acquiring a very useful prop to draw potential customers. As Spider fought and struggled gamely, spreading grime over Mr Gilson's clothes, the caretaker said in a harsh voice, 'You'd better stop that. You're not going anywhere except where *I* choose.'

At the end of school Miss Potter had time to think constructively about the monkey. All afternoon the children had bombarded her with questions about him. 'Has he been caught?' 'What's going to happen to him?' 'Where did he come from?' She had told them to concentrate on their lessons; that they would find out about the monkey tomorrow. But now, with her own mind freed from the need to concentrate on the matters in hand, she was eager to know herself just what had happened. As the children left for home, running towards their parents with news of the most exciting event of the day, she walked quickly round to the caretaker's house.

Gilson had made sure the monkey was hidden well out of sight and hearing. He was ready for Miss Potter's enquiry. 'No, I'm afraid I couldn't get to him,' he answered her untruthfully. 'The roof wouldn't bear my weight so I tried to coax him down. But he didn't want to know. He ran off and climbed down the drainpipe. And that was the last I saw of him.'

The teacher had no reason to doubt Gilson's word even though she didn't like the man's surly manners. 'What a shame,' she said with feeling. 'Someone must be missing him. And he can't survive for long on his own.'

'Someone should have looked after him,' Gilson growled in response. He had no feelings of guilt.

Miss Potter left. She knew there would be a lot of disappointed children the next day. The Stickells children were going to be the most disappointed of all. They had as good as told their mother that the 'monkey who had come to our house' had been captured at school.

As soon as the coast was clear, Mr Gilson fetched Spider from the wood shed where he had locked him up. He had put a loop of string round one of the monkey's arms so that he could lead him about without getting too close and running the risk of being bitten. He pulled the unwilling animal after him back into the cottage and gave Spider some biscuits to eat. He was no expert on the macaque diet. Spider didn't show a lot of interest. He was frightened and looked very downcast.

When the caretaker judged that his brother-in-law would be indoors he telephoned him.

'That you, Bob? I've got a proposition for you.' He offered Spider to the photographer for one hundred pounds. The photographer laughed. He suggested fifty.

'Seventy-five,' said Gilson.

'Sixty,' said the photographer whose name was Fraser.

'Seventy,' said Gilson.

'Sixty-five. And I want to see him first.'

'All right. He's yours to collect.'

'Me collect? That'll cost me in petrol on top of the sixty-five!'

'It's only sixteen miles, for heaven's sake. I don't want to be seen with the beast. I've put it round that he escaped.'

'OK, when shall I come?'

'The sooner the better. I want to be shot of him.'

'Tonight then?'

'Perfect.'

Fraser arrived after dark. He was a short tubby man with a bald head. Gilson had put Spider in a stout cardboard carton. The monkey hadn't much room but he was too dispirited to do anything but sit in the box, quaking fearfully. Gilson opened it up gingerly. Fraser stared.

'He's filthy!' he exclaimed.

'Yeah. He fell down the chimney.'

'And you've just left him like that? How do you know he wasn't injured?' Fraser wasn't completely heartless.

'Couldn't have been,' Gilson answered gruffly. 'You should've seen how he struggled.'

'You might have cleaned him up a bit, poor thing.'

'Not me. He bites.'

'I'm not surprised.'

Spider turned a miserable gaze up at the two men. Fraser felt a modicum of pity. 'Where did he come from?'

'I told you – I don't know. Don't want to, either.'

'Have you fed him at all?'

'I gave him some biscuits. He didn't seem very interested.'

'Biscuits! He's not a dog, he's a monkey. They like bananas and things. Fruit; you know.'

Gilson sighed impatiently. 'Do you want him or not?'

'Not for sixty-five pounds, I don't. Not in that condition, John. I'll give you fifty.'

'Look, Bob, you said—'

'Never mind what I said. I hadn't seen him then, had I?'

'Think of the extra business you'll get. People love animals, don't they?'

'Some of them.' Fraser smiled thinly. 'Fifty pounds to take him off your hands. And I don't know what Margot will say.' Margot was Gilson's sister.

Gilson shrugged. 'None of her business,' he said.

'Of course it's her business. We'll have to keep him in the house.'

'What's wrong with the garage?'

'No. Wouldn't be big enough. I've got to make him a cage.'

Gilson shut the carton with resignation. 'Right. Give me the money and take him away.'

Fraser counted out the notes. 'I hope this doesn't backfire on me,' he said. 'There you are.' He handed them over. 'I'm off then.' He picked up the box. 'I'll see you, John.'

'Yeah. See you.'

Bob Fraser carried Spider to the car. The monkey bounced about, chattering to himself in the most extreme agitation. Half an hour later they arrived at the seaside town of Litton. Spider was taken indoors.

'I've been to see John,' Fraser told his wife.

'Oh yes? What's he palmed on to you this time?'

'You'll never guess. Look what he found today.' He opened the box a fraction.

'Whatever is it?'

'It's a monkey, Margot.'

'A monkey! You're kidding me.'

'No, I'm not. Here, have a closer look. It turned up at the school from nowhere.'

'What on earth do we want it for?' Margot cried crossly.

'Well, he couldn't keep it there, could he? So I—'

'So you volunteered to relieve him of it! Whatever's it got all over it?'

'Soot, I suppose. It fell down the chimney. And I didn't volunteer anything. John rang me up and asked if I could use it – you know, for photography.'

'And he didn't even give it a wash first?' Margot shouted. 'Yes, it sounds just like my brother. And you, too,' she added in a derogatory tone. She glared at him. 'All right – how much did you pay?'

'Oh – not a lot.'

'I bet. You're a mug, Bob.'

'I only paid half of what he asked. And it *could* earn us quite a bit. It'll certainly attract people, won't it?'

'Oh yes, I'm sure it will in that state!'

'Don't be silly, Margot. We're not going to leave him like this. We'll have to wash him and – and—'

'What's this "we"?' she interrupted shrilly. 'You don't think I'm doing it, do you? Because I'm not. And where are we going to keep it?' She softened a bit. 'Poor little brute. He's terrified.'

'Oh, he'll soon feel at home.' Fraser closed the carton. 'I'll give him a bath. Then I'll feed him. Have we got any bananas?'

Washed (despite his struggles), dried and groomed by a not unfriendly pair of hands, Spider had been able to relax a little. His suspicions of Fraser were, to some degree, allayed. At least he could tell he was not going to be ill-treated. He ate some of the fruit offered to him in a careful manner. Margot Fraser was quite taken with his new appearance.

'Oh, he looks all fluffy,' she said. 'Quite a different picture. He could be quite sweet if treated nicely.'

'That's what I mean to do,' said Fraser. 'I'm going to train him.' He held Spider in his arms. The monkey made no attempt to free himself. His recent ordeal had exhausted him.

119

'Where are you going to put him?'

'That's the problem. Until I've made a strong cage for him there isn't really anywhere suitable.'

'Well, you can't just allow him free range,' Margot said pointedly. 'Think of the furniture.'

'I am,' said her husband. 'Can you suggest anything?'

'Of course I can't. I didn't ask for him to be brought here!'

'No, no, all right. Well, there's only one thing for it then. It'll have to be the car.'

'The *car*?'

'Yes, it's ideal. He can't do any damage in there. I'll put some old rugs and things in it. He can snuggle up in those. And I'll leave him some food in case he gets hungry during the night.'

'Mind you give him some air,' Margot Fraser said thoughtfully. 'We don't want to find a dead monkey in the morning, especially after what you paid for him.'

'You don't know what I paid for him.'

'I can guess.'

'Of course he'll have air,' Fraser replied. 'I'll wind a window down a little. It'll be nice and quiet for him in the garage. He'll settle down quite quickly there.'

He couldn't have been more wrong. As soon as Spider smelt the car he was reminded of his recent terrifying experience; his manhandling by Gilson and the horrible confinement in the box on the journey to Litton. He started to utter shrill cries of fear and, as the string had long ago been removed by Fraser, it was as much as the man could do to prevent Spider's escape. He hugged the animal to his chest in

120

a vice-like grip, bundled him into the car and shut the door. Spider leapt from seat to seat in a frantic attempt to find an escape route, still shrieking his alarm. Fraser hurried back for some soft covers for the seats and some more fruit.

'This'll quieten him down,' he murmured to himself as he showed Spider the bananas.

Spider wasn't in the least interested in food. He was in a highly-strung state. Fraser got in the car and tried to calm him. He spread the rugs and cloths around, talking all the while in a quiet voice.

Spider perched on top of the driver's head-rest and regarded him unhappily. He was trembling from head to foot. Fraser tried to persuade him to look at a banana. Spider bared his teeth in misery and perplexity. Fraser thought he was risking being bitten and decided Spider would be better left alone to calm himself. He let down one window just a fraction and then quickly got out. As soon as the door was shut on him again Spider resumed his frenzied leaping about.

With many misgivings about possible injuries to the monkey, Fraser went back indoors. He tried to tell himself that Spider would wear himself out eventually but he was distinctly uneasy about the situation.

'Is he all right?' his wife asked at once.

'Oh yes,' Fraser lied. 'He'll be OK, he's just a bit excited at the moment.'

'The sooner you make him something permanent the better,' Margot remarked. 'What are you going to make it from, Bob?'

'Wood, of course.'

'Will it be strong enough?'

121

'Of course it will. He's not a gorilla, is he?'

'No, but the only monkeys I've seen have been behind bars.'

Fraser pulled a face at her. 'This isn't a zoo,' he said irritably. 'And the whole point is, I don't want him to be behind *anything* most of the time. I want him out with me on my patch.' He fell silent, wondering how long the monkey would continue to jump about. He began to think the whole idea was perhaps not such a good one after all.

—14—

Black Water

Pie hid amongst the logs until dark. He knew the cat was somewhere about. He couldn't see it or smell it, he just knew it in his bones. He also knew Thrifty had been captured. During the day he heard Auntie's squawking calls from time to time but he stayed quiet and remained where he was. He didn't know how he would outwit the cat and get away but he knew there was also no chance of his doing so in the daylight. He licked his fur and nursed his hurts. He had two small bald patches where his coat had been badly burnt.

Auntie had not entirely given up on the animals. She kept searching and calling. She didn't dare believe they had been burned alive in the bonfire and by the time this was just a mass of grey glowing embers she was no longer afraid to go near it. The cat watched the parrot with interest. The animal felt that now there were two possibilities of a catch, although it recognized Auntie was a large bird. Really its hunting abilities were more suited to pouncing on a rat.

Dusk began to fall. It had been a cloudy day and the evening grew very dark. Still Pie waited, afraid to move. He was safe in the log pile but he knew he couldn't stay there indefinitely. His whiskers trembled. He felt very lonely. He wondered if Auntie was still in the vicinity. He would have loved to have had the comfort of knowing a friend – any friend – was nearby, but he guessed the parrot would be sleeping by now. At last he edged very slowly out of the protection of the wood stack, carefully ensuring his body made not the slightest rustle. His nose twitched nervously as he tested the air. He couldn't smell the cat. He paused to look about for his next place of shelter, intending to go from cover to cover in short quick bursts of running. He was very fast on his feet and he thought this was his best plan of action. There was a Lawson's cypress on one side of the garden. It seemed, with its thick foliage growing almost from ground level, to be a good place to make for. Pie realized that it was quite a long run for him. However, there was simply nothing else.

He didn't hesitate too long. Abruptly he dashed out, running just as fast as he possibly could. The cat seemed not to be in evidence. Pie fled to the dark screen of perfumed vegetation. Soon he was underneath it, panting with relief. All at once he heard Auntie's voice screech from the boughs of the cypress.

'The cat, Pie! The cat!'

He glanced around. Even as he did so he was pinned down by a tremendous weight. The cunning hunter had been waiting upwind of him.

The cat's claws pierced his flesh. In a moment, Pie knew, all would be over. He waited fatalistically for the savage bite that would paralyse him. But Auntie, thoroughly alarmed herself by the sudden appearance of the cat, began to fire off corks one after the other. The cat froze, unable to detect the source of the noise. Auntie's telephone rang next. 'BRRR. BRRR. HELLO WINDMILL PET SHOP. NUTS. HAVE ANOTHER ONE MADAM. THANK YOU. POP! POP!'

The cat sprang away, unnerved by the strange human sounds that came mysteriously out of the dark empty garden. Pie scuttled away the instant the pressure of the cruel claws was released and buried himself under a thick pile of dead brown cypress leaves that lay at the base of the tree. Auntie screeched twice at the top of her voice. It was an eerie, ringing cry. The cat bolted. It suddenly lost interest in the thrills of the hunt and wanted reassurance. It ran to the cottage and miaowed to be let in.

'Cat's gone, cat's gone!' cried Auntie triumphantly. 'Pie's safe. Cat's gone!'

'He'll be back,' Pie answered, peeping out of the leaf litter. 'I know cats. I'd better make the most of his absence now!' He dashed away again, ignoring the smarting wounds inflicted on him by the cat's claws. In the darkness he was invisible to Auntie who was unable to follow his progress. She had no way of showing him where to go. However, Pie had no thought any more for the windmill. All he could think of was how to get himself into a deep dark hole well beyond the reach of any cat.

The garden didn't seem to provide any such refuge. He went further, seeking desperately for a permanent shelter. How foolish he and Thrifty had been to think that anything above ground like the rubbish was safe. Only a hole below the surface, where nothing could penetrate, was really secure. He ran on, afraid that at any moment the cat would be back on his track. He could almost feel the crushing weight of its next pounce driving every breath from his body. He knew he wouldn't escape again. If there was another pounce it would be the last. Pie had no idea that the cat was now comfortably settled indoors, curled up on a favourite chair.

A little later, he thought he had found what he was looking for. He was in another enclosure that ran alongside the garden. He came to a spot bare of grass. There was a round wooden lid lying flush with the ground in which an inviting hole had been cut. It was just wide enough for a small animal to squeeze through.

'This is the place,' Pie told himself with relief. 'Only an animal like me or Thrifty could get in there.' He confidently believed the hole was the entrance to an underground tunnel. How was he to know he was standing on a well cover? The pulley system with its mounting and handle, which was next to the hole, meant nothing to him. But he did find a chain running through the hole in the wooden lid.

'There's still room for me to slip inside,' he told himself. He hadn't a clue what the chain was as he'd never seen one close up before. He pushed his head through the hole. At once he was enveloped in the cavernous blackness of the brick-lined well. Of course he couldn't see the bottom and, in the darkness, he couldn't see the sides either.

'Perfect!' he squeaked. 'No threat in here. All quiet and still.' He wriggled through the gap, grasping the

126

chain with his front paws. 'Now, then, where's the path?' He peered about, wrinkling his nose; his whiskers twitching. Next he clutched the hanging chain with his hind paws, winding his long tail round it for extra grip. His front paws were free now to test the void of blackness for a firm foundation. But they found only empty space.

'Hm, strange!' Pie muttered, 'Wherever have I got myself? I can't seem to find the way through at all.' He pulled back and examined the chain. 'This must lead somewhere, I suppose.' He began to climb down the chain, slowly and carefully, using all four feet. His skinny tail acted as a perfect counterbalance. The chain went on . . . and on . . . and on . . . Pie began to feel a little nervous. 'This isn't a proper path,' he murmured. Every so often he paused to test either side of the twisting metal chain that quivered and swung with his every movement. Each time his paws encountered nothing solid: nothing to hold, nothing to step on to. At the outset his keen sense of smell had detected the unmistakable scent of water. As he descended, so this smell became stronger. 'There must be a path eventually,' Pie reassured himself. 'I expect it'll go around the water.'

Later he nearly slipped and he paused as the chain rippled and swung precariously. 'I – I don't like this,' he squealed. 'Where am I going?' But there was no alternative. He had to press on.

The chain wound down for more than five metres. Towards the bottom it became very slippery. Moss and slime had collected on it; the well hadn't been used for years. Pie swayed and nearly lost his grip. The atmosphere was cold and dank. He was afraid.

'This was a mistake, coming in here,' he decided. 'There's a sort of menace about the place. I'd better not go on. I'll climb back up and get out again.' But it wasn't as simple as that. It was very difficult trying to change his position on the chain from a downward direction to an upward one. He had to try and turn his body on the slippery metal links with – just for a second – only his hind paws still gripping. And in that second he lost his balance. He slid down, his front paws beating the air in his attempt to grasp on to the swinging chain. Finally, with a horribly cold, echoing splash, he fell into the water. Pie was a good swimmer. But the water was terribly cold and he could see absolutely nothing. He panicked, paddling frantically round and round the cylindrical construction, vainly endeavouring to find something to grip, to climb on to. He only succeeded in bumping his nose against the brick lining.

'Calm yourself, Pie. Calm yourself,' he muttered. 'You're going round in circles. Ugh! This water's so cold.' He allowed his body to float momentarily as he tried to think how to save himself. 'I've got to get back to that thing I was on before. That's my only hope.' He drifted to the centre of the well and came up against a solid object which was below the water. His body had struck the bucket which lay submerged on the end of the chain. His feet scrabbled for a hold but the bucket was too deep down. It was no use to him. He swam some more. The chain eluded him. His limbs tired and the bitter cold of the water began to dull his senses.

Outside the well and back in the garden Auntie tucked her head under her wing. She hadn't moved

128

from the cypress tree. 'I'll look for Pie in the morning,' she told herself. 'I must find him — otherwise what do I do next?'

Since her lucky escapes from the bonfire and the garden rake, Thrifty the hamster had been treated well. Mrs Grice fed and watered her and when she was in Wandle the next day she went to the Windmill Pet Shop with her notice.

'Can you help?' she asked Dobson, holding out a slip of paper. 'I've found a hamster and I've no idea where it came from.'

Dobson's ears pricked up. 'A hamster?' he glanced at the paper. 'What colour?'

'It's a golden hamster.'

'Ah-ha. And were there other animals with it?'

'Other animals? No. As a matter of fact it must have been sleeping in our rubbish pile. We only found it when my husband decided to have a bonfire.'

Dobson winced. 'Was it injured?'

'Only a little. I'm afraid my husband thought it was a rat at first and he would have killed it. But I managed to save it. And actually, there *was* a rat in the pile as well. So you see—'

'I thought you said there weren't any other animals?' Dobson interrupted sharply. He was certain now that the hamster was Thrifty.

Mrs Grice gaped. 'But surely,' she said, 'you weren't referring to horrible creatures like rats?'

'I may have been,' Dobson replied. 'I've lost one — a pet rat, of course. *And* a hamster. And a monkey. And a tortoise. And a parrot.'

'Oh dear,' said Mrs Grice. 'How upsetting. But a

129

monkey? No, I haven't seen that, or the others. I didn't think – the rat, I suppose could have been. . . . We weren't to know. . . . I mean, a rat is a rat, isn't it?' She sounded uncertain.

'Was it black and white?'

Mrs Grice racked her memory. 'There *may* have been some white on it,' she conceded.

'I'm sure the animals are mine,' Dobson pronounced. He went on to explain how he had already retrieved Candyfloss and Skip. He arranged with Mrs Grice to collect Thrifty.

'Don't trouble to come all the way out,' said the lady, who was feeling a little bit guilty. 'I can bring the little animal in tomorrow.'

'No, no,' Dobson said, 'it's early closing today. I'll come this afternoon. Then I can look for the rat, too. Er – you didn't see any evidence of a parrot, I suppose?'

Mrs Grice was sure on that point. 'Definitely no parrot. We get all sorts of birds in the garden and I'd know if a parrot had been around!'

'No sound of one?'

'I haven't been listening out. There are so many different birds' cries, aren't there?'

'A parrot's is quite unlike any native bird's,' Dobson pointed out.

'Exactly. So I would have noticed it, wouldn't I?'

'Not if you weren't listening out,' Dobson remarked with a wintry smile.

Pie was exhausted. He had swum around for ages, his movements becoming progressively sluggish and hopeless. He was numbed by the icy water and when

130

at last his snout nudged the chain it was as much as he could do to catch hold of it with his front paws and haul himself out. There he hung, dripping black water and aching with cold, unable to move any further. His whole frame shook uncontrollably. Only his wounds ceased to hurt since his body was so numbed. Yet he knew he must climb all the way back up that chain, slippery link by slippery link, or face certain death by drowning, for if he ever tumbled back into the water it would be the end of him.

He clung on grimly. At length, some of the effect of the cold wore off and he began, very shakily, to climb. One centimetre, two centimetres. . . . Pie pulled himself up. It was a laborious process in his weakened state. And he got slower and slower. He began to see he wouldn't make it. He no longer had the strength to get right to the top. With trembling paws he continued to grip the chain. Below him lay the black icy water and above him an impossible climb of several metres to the open air and freedom.

—— 15 ——

Auntie in Doubt

The next morning Auntie fluttered from her bower in the scented fir tree. She made a hasty visit to the maize field and ate some more corn. She intended to tell Pie about it when she found him. She was determined that he would be found, particularly now that Spider had disappeared. She flew over the area, calling. Of course the rat made no reply. From his self-imposed imprisonment he heard the parrot squawking and screeching his name. The last vestiges of strength were leaving him and he couldn't have managed more than a gasp even if he had had the vain hope that he would be heard. But he didn't. He had no hope of anything. He waited only for that inevitable moment when he would lose his grip and plunge like a stone to the well bottom. He wondered where Thrifty was and he thought about their tiny cages in the pet shop – so cluttered, yet so safe.

A little later, as Auntie continued her fruitless search for her companion, she saw the Grices' black cat once more stepping fastidiously across the garden. The animal hadn't forgotten the rat it had caught and then allowed to escape and it went directly to the cypress, remembering where it had been diverted from making its kill. The scent of Pie was strong under the tree's boughs. The cat started to search more deliberately. Auntie kept clear. But she thought she oughtn't to keep too far away in case her ability to mimic should be needed again. She had saved Pie once and she certainly wouldn't hesitate to do so again.

'The cat may even be of use,' she said to herself. 'It's closer to the ground than I am. Maybe it'll unearth Pie before I can.'

Mrs Grice had unconsciously been listening to bird calls ever since she had got back home. Her husband had told her he had heard some unusual ones while she had been out.

'Couldn't have been a parrot, I suppose?' she mused. 'There's a parrot missing.'

'A parrot! Now I wonder!' he answered. 'I looked out once or twice but I saw nothing definite. They were strong, carrying cries, though, that I heard. Rather like a crow or rook, only more high-pitched like. A parrot, eh? Well, you never know.'

'The man's coming later. Perhaps he'll hear them.'

Auntie was holding her peace as she watched the cat. It seemed to her to have no particular plan in mind, wandering round in a casual sort of way. However, when it got into the neighbouring enclosure it became excited. Its tail started to swish ominously. Auntie wondered if it was on Pie's trail. The cat proceeded along the ground, pausing frequently to sniff. It came to the well head. Its tail switched to and fro. It peered into the hole in the well cover and miaowed with satisfaction. It was a menacing miaow. Pie heard it and shivered violently. The cat knew he was there. Surreptitiously Auntie flew closer.

At this moment, Joel Dobson's van drew up outside the Grices' cottage. The black cat heard voices but it was too absorbed in its discovery to do more than cock an ear. Mrs Grice took Dobson inside. Thrifty was produced and the old man claimed her.

'Well, well!' he said delightedly. 'I never expected to see you again. And all neatly bandaged too. You have been well tended.'

'I'm so pleased to find the rightful owner,' said Mrs Grice. 'I never thought I would. The little animal's all right, you know. She was only scratched.' A thought struck her. 'Oh, by the way,' she went on, 'my husband has heard some strange bird calls this morning, he says. If you come this way he'll tell you all about them.'

'I'll just put Thrifty in the van,' Dobson said, 'and I'll be with you.'

Five minutes later he was in the Grices' garden, straining his ears and eyes for Auntie. Pie was out of his mind for the moment. The parrot could see her owner quite clearly from her perch in the shrubbery close to the well. She was sorely tempted to fly over and sit on his shoulder. But she stayed where she was, silent and still. Somehow, she felt, the business of the windmill had to be resolved. Once that was over she could fly home whenever she chose. She was nicely hidden from view and Dobson eventually walked right past her.

'Can you hear those calls now?' he asked Mr Grice. 'I can't pick out anything unusual.'

134

'No, not now,' came the reply. 'It was earlier I heard them, y'see. Perhaps the bird's gone – whatever it was.'

Dobson looked exasperated. 'Well, if you do hear anything again,' he said gruffly, 'let me know.' He thought about Pie and, at that instant, the black cat caught his attention. There was something about the animal's pose – frozen into immobility, yet watchful and eager – that looked worth investigating. 'Your cat's found something there,' he remarked. 'Is that a well?'

'Yes, not used though; not for years.'

'I don't suppose I could have a look?'

'Course you can. You help yourself. You won't find anything down there, I shouldn't think.'

'I'm not so sure,' Dobson murmured and ducked under the wire fence. He advanced on the well. The black cat wavered and finally scampered away. Dobson dug two fingers in the hole in the lid and prised it up. Light flooded into the well, blinding Pie who was still there, gripping the chain, in spite of his waning powers. Grice came up.

'There's something on the chain,' said Dobson. 'I can't quite see – it's certainly a rat. Have you a torch handy?'

Grice stumped away and presently returned with the required article. He handed it to the other man. Dobson shone it directly on to the animal. Pie, scorched, soaked and bedraggled, was nevertheless recognizable to his owner.

'No doubt about it,' said Dobson curtly. 'He's mine.' He turned and began to heave on the lever. The chain started to move. Pie clung on with difficulty. The bucket emerged from the water as Dobson wound the handle, water gushing from its brim. Slowly, slowly, Pie neared the surface. He was all but spent.

Grice watched the proceedings with some surprise. He couldn't for the life of him understand all this fuss over a rat. 'You going to catch him if he jumps out?' he asked dubiously as Pie was swung up the last few centimetres.

Dobson ceased turning. He bent down and, just as his hands were about to close on his pet rat, Pie's last ounce of strength was used up. He slipped away, back down into the depths but this time only as far as the bucket which caught him neatly. Dobson bent to the lever again. The bucket came up with Pie spreadeagled and floating on the water inside. Dobson fished him out.

'Another patient for your wife's administrations, I think,' the shop owner remarked to the amazed onlooker. 'It looks as if we got to him just in time.'

Auntie watched the two men return to the cottage. 'Now what?' she muttered. 'There's another one who'll never get to the windmill.'

Of all the pets, Pebble was the most dogged. There was a sort of grim determination about his reptilian plod that nothing living or otherwise could deter. He just kept going forward at his own pace, confident that eventually – no matter how long it might take him – he would turn up at the required place. He had a rendezvous and he meant to keep it.

To the tortoise it seemed he had already travelled a tremendous distance. In fact he had only just reached

136

the arable field where Skip had been terrified by the harvester. Pebble fondly imagined himself to be almost up to the point where he might catch sight of one of his old companions.

'I wonder what they'll say when they see me?' he mused as he trudged along. 'I must be close now. And I don't have to sleep as much as they do. I can keep going – night or day. I wonder if they'll be surprised? I hope they'll be pleased. It's been rather a lonely trek, this.'

Of course Pebble hadn't been entirely alone. True to their word Speckle and Wart had reappeared at odd times to mark his progress and keep him company. As the tortoise went further afield their appearances became less frequent. They didn't care to pass too far beyond the bounds of their own little world.

'He's a great traveller,' Speckle remarked as they saw Pebble lumbering on.

'He has a goal, hasn't he?' said Wart. 'I suppose he'll know when he attains it?'

'Must do, I should think. Otherwise he'll travel for ever.'

'Well, he knows the name of the place. That's something.'

'Yes, it is,' Speckle agreed. 'Er – I suppose we don't need to actually go the *whole* way with him, do we?'

'On no account,' said Wart.

'I mean, it could be just about anywhere really, this windmill.'

'Of course it could.'

'Shall we catch him up and wish him well?'

'I don't know,' said Wart. 'He's quite a long way

ahead, isn't he? Perhaps we'll catch him on the way back.'

'Oh yes, that's it. On the way back. I say – I'm starving, aren't you?'

'Ravenous,' replied Wart.

Like a clockwork toy that never runs down Pebble blundered on. There was always sufficient food for him everywhere he went and, besides, he didn't need to eat every day. His thoughts were certainly turned to other things than food when, to his amazement and pleasure, he spied Skip – or something very like Skip – feeding along the hedgerow. He was able to get within a short distance before the rabbit looked up. Pebble's hopes were dashed. He could see plainly now it wasn't Skip after all. Yet there was certainly a resemblance.

The rabbit sat and watched him for a while. Then it came towards him inquisitively. It was apparent that it found Pebble very puzzling.

'I thought you were a friend of mine at first,' the tortoise said in his slow voice by way of introduction.

The rabbit seemed astonished that he had a voice at all. 'A – a friend?' it repeated. 'But how could I be? I've never seen anything—'

'I know,' Pebble interrupted. 'I know what you're going to say. You've never seen anything quite like me before. I'm getting used to such remarks. But I don't know why; I'm just an ordinary everyday tortoise. Nothing strange about me. And, you see, I *know* what you are, because I have a friend who looks like you.'

'Another rabbit?'

'Of course another rabbit, otherwise he wouldn't

look like you, would he? I haven't seen him in a very long while. And I thought. . . . But there we are, I was wrong.'

The rabbit suddenly took on the look of something that has all at once discovered the clue to a mystery. He was quite excited. 'I think I've seen your friend,' he said quickly. 'Is he called Skip?'

'Well – yes. How did you—'

The rabbit was none other than Fleet who had helped Skip escape from the harvesting. 'I thought as much. He came this way, you know. We had an adventure together, but he went on his way. He didn't want to come into the warren. He was on some sort of journey.'

'That's right!'

'Yes, and he told me about some other animals who were going the same way. And you're one of them, aren't you, and you're all going to meet up somewhere at the end of the journey?'

'That's it exactly,' said Pebble. 'But I haven't seen any of the others yet. How long is it since Skip came past?'

'Oh, a long time back. I'd almost forgotten him.'

'Yes, yes, I'd guessed as much,' said Pebble fatalistically. 'I'm so much slower, of course. You can see that.'

'I did notice it,' Fleet admitted. 'I wasn't quite sure at first if you were moving at all.'

'Huh! I know,' Pebble returned, 'that's the way of it. We tortoises *are* slow but we're also persistent.'

'Well, we're all different, aren't we?' Fleet remarked for something to say. 'I don't know if I can be of any help to you.'

'None at all. None at all. But thank you. And – yes, you have been of help. At least I know my friends are ahead of me. I don't expect you've seen any of the others?'

'I believe not,' Fleet replied. 'Are they rabbits?'

'No.'

'I haven't, then.'

'Ah, well, on to the windmill.'

'The windmill! I remember. Skip talked of it. Good luck to you – er – tortoise. Tell Skip you saw me.'

'I will,' said Pebble.

'There you are, Eric. There's the two of them.'

'Thank you, Mr Dobson.'

Eric took Thrifty and Pie, much cleaned up and in their little cage, from Joel Dobson. It was the evening of the day when they had been collected from the Grices' property. Eric's searches for Auntie and Spider were abandoned. They had produced nothing concrete and both he and Dobson were of a mind that, as the other animals had been recovered as a result of receiving outside reports, it was just as likely this would be the way of it with the others. Now Eric was to begin working again in the shop, past antagonisms forgotten. He had volunteered to take the hamster and rat to his own home to cosset them and restore them to full health as a recompense for the suffering he felt he had caused them. Dobson had told him to keep them.

'It's a funny thing, isn't it,' Eric remarked, 'that we should have retrieved all the smallest animals? You'd expect the larger ones to be more conspicuous.'

'It's very odd,' Dobson agreed. 'I do wish Auntie

140

would come back. I really miss her and all her clever voices. And I know she was nearby when I went to see Mrs Grice. You'd have thought she'd have come to me.' He sounded quite upset. 'As for Spider . . . well. . . .' He shrugged as if he was beyond guessing what could have happened to the monkey.

Pie and Thrifty lay quietly at the bottom of their comfortable cage. They were warm and dry, they had all their favourite delicacies in a little dish, and they enjoyed the sense of each other's presence. Pie hadn't yet got over the trauma of the deep dark well. He was unusually still and inactive. But he was revelling in the comparative comfort of captivity after such a nightmare and neither he nor Thrifty had any regrets at their recapture.

Auntie stayed around the Grices' cottage a long time. She was irresolute as to her next course of action. Should she go on to the windmill alone? But that would miss the point of the whole episode of the pets' stay in the outside world. The intention had been for them all to gather there together, yet that was no longer possible. Most of the animals' brief flirtation with freedom was over and they were back where they started. And, after all, what had that freedom cost them – uncertainty at the very least, futile wanderings and, worst of all, fear and suffering. Why did she – Auntie – remain loose a moment longer? She had never been the prime mover in the adventure. She had seen the fabled windmill, had discovered something of its secret (or so she thought) and what more was there for her to do? Why shouldn't she fly back to the shop; to her familiar surroundings, unexciting though they may be? Her master had always treated her rather better than some of the smaller creatures. She'd never been confined. Auntie was almost of a mind to do just that. She had accomplished her part of the mission, insofar as there had been a mission in the first place. Certainly she had never been entirely clear about that. It had never been her idea. The idea had been initiated by Spider and she had simply followed along with it like the rest of them.

And that was the problem: Spider. Spider was still loose. Did he still have a trick or two he hadn't revealed? Was there something she didn't know about; something she would never know about if she didn't follow his plan through to the end? Well, to do that she needed to find Spider himself. To accompany him from now on, without any deviation, until they could arrive together. Then, and only then, would she know. Without Spider she was in a sort of limbo. Wherever had he gone? And why hadn't she kept up with him before? Well, it was too late to bemoan that. If she was going to continue on the outside (that's how she saw the countryside as opposed to the 'inside' of the shop) she must find him, and as quickly as possible.

'He can't be so far away,' she reasoned with herself. 'And then, I have the benefit of flight; the other animals have no such advantage. If I can't locate him from the air, then nobody can.' She had cheered herself up and now she was ready to implement her decision. 'Spider, here I come!' she squawked. 'HELLO AUNTIE. CAN I HELP YOU MADAM? GOOD OLD GIRL!'

——16——

Spider's Training

Spider spent the most miserable of nights in Fraser's car. He hated the smell of it, the feel of it, everything about it. The rugs the man had provided were no comfort to him; neither were the bananas any solace. Everything had happened so quickly since he had gambolled on the school roof that he didn't know what had hit him. His acute mental anguish and the strange hostile environment at last tired him out. He passed the nocturnal hours with his face pressed sadly against the car window. He tried to get as close as possible to the narrow space at the top where the only free air that he was permitted entered the vehicle. In the morning Fraser found him there, half dozing, neither asleep nor awake. The bananas were untouched.

'Dear, dear,' the man muttered, 'you don't look at all happy, my friend. You're not going to be much of an asset to me if you go around looking like that. We're going to have to cheer you up.'

He unlocked the car on the opposite side and reached in for the monkey. Spider came willingly enough, he was so desperate to get out. Besides, he had already surmised that Fraser meant him no actual harm.

'I'm going to build you your own home,' said the photographer. 'It'll be in the warm, near us – you won't have any cause to mope then.' He had the sense to realize that it was very much in his interest to look after Spider's well-being. He had got his wife to telephone a small local zoo to enquire about dietary needs.

Inside the house he offered Spider a bowl of warm milk. The monkey appeared to be gratified with it, accepting it readily. He sat on the kitchen table with Margot Fraser keeping an eye on him. He was in no hurry to explore or even to exercise his limbs. His eyes were half closed, he felt very sleepy. Fraser had put a mild sedative in the milk.

All that day Fraser sawed and planed and hammered the timber he had bought for Spider's cage. He was quite a handy man and, late in the afternoon, he put the finishing touches to it. He stood back, assessing its effectiveness. He was very pleased with his efforts. The cage was rectangular; two metres in height and a metre and a half across. The depth was a little over a metre. There were wooden slats at the back and Fraser had fitted chicken wire in to the other three sides. He had fixed a shelf to the interior two thirds of the way up and on this he had constructed a large box with an entrance hole. Inside the box were wood shavings, straw, balls of paper and pieces of cloth. He supposed Spider would make some sort of nest for himself and Fraser meant to familiarize himself in due course with the animal's exact requirements in this respect. He had made

Spider a little ladder to lead up to the shelf. Fraser had ideas of introducing playthings and exercise bars at a later stage. The chief requirement at present was to have something ready to house Spider in time for the rekindling of his naturally lively temperament. The man sprinkled a thick coating of sawdust on the bottom of the cage and made doubly sure all the wood in the interior was rubbed down to a smooth finish with no suggestion of a splinter.

Margot Fraser was delighted with the result of her husband's labours. 'Well, he couldn't have hoped for a better job, could he?' she enthused. 'Let's introduce him to it.'

Spider, still in his languid state, was carried from the kitchen to Fraser's workroom. Fraser opened the latch on the wire front and deposited Spider on the sawdust-covered floor. Spider sat and looked at him, blinking drowsily. Fraser fetched fruit, raw vegetables, water and a small container of cold boiled rice. He locked the cage. Then he and Margot stood and watched, waiting for a reaction. Spider stared back at them and yawned.

'I hope you didn't put too much of that stuff in his milk,' Margot remarked doubtfully.

'Of course not,' Fraser replied. 'It was just a smattering. He'll come round soon.'

'How are you going to train him, Bob?'

'Shouldn't be too difficult. I think he trusts me. A little kindness, a little firmness – you know . . . .'

'Well, I hope he earns back that money you paid for him.'

'That *is* the idea, Margot.'

*

Over the next few days Spider became accustomed to his cage. Fraser had made it really quite comfortable. It was kept tidy and clean and it was always warm. Spider had plenty of variety in his food and, now and again, new items of interest were added with which the monkey could pass the time whilst he was shut up. Playthings – a rubber tyre, a ball, bars to swing from – were incorporated into his new home. Spider loathed it. He had got used to being free and unfettered and he had revelled in the opportunities for exploration and amusement in the open. Most of all he yearned for the windmill. He thought occasionally of his old companions and fumed at the idea that they might have reached their objective without him. For there could be no acceptance there for them without his being there too.

Fraser and his wife were kindly enough – probably as kind as Dobson had ever been – and they seemed to pay him more attention. But Spider was frustrated at being locked up again and he didn't enjoy the long sessions with Fraser when the man tried to teach him tricks. Spider knew all about tricks. He would have been an arch-perpetrator of tricks given half the chance. But *he* wanted to be the one to invent them. He objected to being forced to do things that bored him. He was unco-operative in the extreme until Fraser lost his temper and then he quickly put matters right by doing everything expected of him with ease so that he would end up being spoiled and petted. However, on the very next occasion, the whole process would be repeated.

'He's so infuriating,' Fraser complained. 'I know he can do all the simple things standing on his head. I don't ask much, after all. But if he's in one of his moods he won't respond to titbits, wheedling or anything. The only thing that gets him going is my shouting.'

One day Gilson got on the phone to find out how things were progressing.

'He's not easy,' Fraser told him.

'Have you been out with him yet?'

'No, no, not yet. I need more time. He's so unpredictable.'

Gilson grunted, 'You want to get tough with him.'

'What's the point of that, John? I don't want him to look cowed.'

'Oh well, you know your business, I suppose.'

It was another week before Spider got his first airing. Fraser chose a fine sunny day. He'd put a collar on Spider and to this he had attached a short chain. Whilst the monkey rode on his shoulders, Fraser walked up and down the promenade at Litton holding on to Spider tightly. Spider understood all about the chain. He wasn't tempted to seek his liberty because he knew just how far the chain would stretch and he also knew the results if he tried to overstretch it. He had suffered several painful and frightening experiences that way already, back in the house. Fraser had taken no equipment with him. He wanted Spider to get used to being walked up and down.

The monkey enjoyed the outing up to a point. It was a change of scene. He liked the opportunity to look around and see other people and what they were doing. His inquisitiveness had never entirely deserted him. But he didn't like the noise of the traffic

147

at all. He was quite unused to that, and the heavy double-decker buses which passed by were particularly frightening. At first he trembled every time one came near.

Fraser was a well-known figure along the sea front. Stallholders and shop owners who had known him for years were intrigued by his new pet. They called out to him. One or two wanted a closer look at the monkey. Spider enjoyed best of all being the centre of attraction. But he intended to make a break from his new unlooked-for master just as soon as he could find a way of doing it.

There were still a good number of holidaymakers about. Fraser was encouraged by the 'ooohs' and 'aahs' of the children as they pointed excitedly to the monkey.

'Oh-ho, you'll be worth your weight in gold before long,' he murmured, half to Spider and half to himself.

The photographer was impatient to begin making use of the monkey. But at the same time he still had to earn his living, so he wasn't able to take Spider with him every day. The monkey wasn't yet sufficiently schooled in his contribution to his master's business and he would have been more of a hindrance than a help.

At home Fraser acquainted Spider with the noise of the camera and got Margot to pose with him on her shoulder for some flash pictures. To begin with, Spider was alarmed by the suddenness of the blinding light but they got round that problem by making sure he always had a banana or an apple or

148

something to divert his attention while the pictures were being taken. It wasn't long before he came to disregard the light altogether. He was quick to learn that it offered him no harm. Sometimes Margot posed with Spider simply cuddled in her arms. He rather liked this – he liked her smell and she was gentle with him. Fraser was also pleased because he wanted Spider to get used to being handled by other people.

All the time his training went on, Spider was on the look out for a means of escape. Indoors, Fraser gave him no opportunity whatsoever. If he wasn't locked in his cage he was held on his chain by Fraser or Margot. It didn't take Spider long to work out that his best hope was when they went outside. He looked forward to these outings for that reason, and gradually they became more regular.

Fraser noticed Spider seemed to enjoy being near people and that he was interested in them. He also knew that he liked to show off, given the smallest opportunity. All this worked to the photographer's advantage and the time came when he was ready to begin putting Spider to use.

It was a clear, warm sunny day. Fraser walked along the promenade with Spider balanced on his shoulder. He stopped by a flower garden, a popular spot for strollers. Spider was allowed to run and jump about to the full extent of his chain. The monkey sensed his additional freedom and exulted in it, bounding about and chattering to himself. Soon a small crowd had gathered. Children were pushed to the front. Some of them asked to pet the monkey. Fraser assured the parents this was quite safe: the animal had never been known to bite. Spider adored all the attention and really played up to the onlookers. Once he made a great leap, landing on Fraser's shoulder, a place he now regarded as a sort of perch. The photographer wasn't expecting it and staggered momentarily. Before he could show his annoyance with the monkey the crowd roared approval. Thereafter Fraser encouraged Spider to repeat the trick which, with a growing audience, he was only too happy to do.

Fraser now made his pitch. 'Come on, folks, come and be photographed with the monkey. Any way you like – he loves to pose. Souvenir of your holiday. A snap of your choice *with* a difference.'

The children were very enthusiastic. Soon Fraser was clicking away at parents holding Spider with their children in front; children standing on their own with Spider sat between them; a pair of teenagers with Spider sitting on the shoulder of one. Business was brisk.

Fraser was delighted. And Spider began to see that, as the photographer allowed him progressively more leeway, there might come an opportunity when the chain would not be in any person's hand. He watched very, very carefully. He knew that it would only take one instant of forgetfulness and he would be off. Freedom beckoned once more and, once free, he'd never be caught again. Spider bided his time and waited for his moment.

Margot was thrilled with her husband's news. 'Oh Bob!' she cried. 'You were right. I never thought it'd work out.' She cooed at Spider. 'Bless him! He really played up to them. He shall have a special treat for that.' And she went off to the kitchen to see what she could find.

Spider rested in his cage from his al fresco performance. He groomed himself pensively. He didn't feel like playing on his own. He thought of the chain and he thought of the windmill: the windmill, the chain, the chain, the windmill. . . .

For many days during Spider's training period Auntie flew hither and thither, searching for him. She flew around the school where she knew he had been attracted by the children's voices. She flew over the terrain they had crossed before. She even flew to the windmill again in case he had managed to come there by some other obscure route. She fed herself where she could on fruit, windfalls, corn and scraps. She even tasted hedgerow berries and twigs. At night she roosted alone and away from other birds in shrubs, trees or creepers. Once she perched on a garage shelf. She saw no sign of Spider. He seemed to have disappeared without trace. She was horribly lonely. She longed for company. She didn't seek companionship amongst other birds especially when, on her return to the windmill, she found the orchard deserted. The blackbirds and thrushes had used up the feeble crop of fruit and were filling their stomachs elsewhere. She didn't feel entirely comfortable amongst small songbirds who eyed her askance.

Occasionally she gave vent to some impressions in an effort to keep her spirits up, but only in a half-hearted way since her audience was confined to one. She began to question her continued subsistence on the English countryside. She saw her daily routine as increasingly pointless. The comfort, the noise, the human bustle and talk of the pet shop exerted its sway. She had nothing with which to resist it because the alternative to the parrot's returning home was one she was unable to define. Spider was lost. Auntie was alone. She tired of the situation.

One evening at dusk she set her face towards Wandle and began her flight back. Eric was sweeping out the shop just after closing. Not for the first time he stopped to lean on his broom and look at the sign on the door. 'The Windmill Pet Shop.' How inappropriate it seemed. There *were* no pets. He wondered if Joel Dobson would agree with him that a change to a more apt name for the premises was timely.

'The Windmill Pet Supplies,' Eric murmured to himself. 'That would be more suitable.' A muffled squawk interrupted his musing. It came from outside. He stepped to the door and looked out. Auntie sat on the fence across the road, calmly preening herself. She raised her head.

'THANK YOU MADAM. AUNTIE PET SHOP. HERE YOU ARE. WINDMILL,' she croaked confusedly. Then she flapped her wings and flew over, straight through the doorway and on to her old stand by the till. It was as if she had only been absent a few hours.

Eric closed the door, open-mouthed. He pulled himself together. 'Mr Dobson!' he called. 'MR DOBSON!'

But he needn't have yelled. Joel Dobson was stumbling downstairs in his slippers, having heard the wonderful sound of popping corks.

——17——

An Enemy Reappears

Fine weather continued almost unabated for the next month. September had been beautiful and the settled period continued on into October. Fraser had made the most of the Indian summer and he and Spider had done very well indeed for the time of year. Now that Litton was reverting to its sleepy winter state there was not enough business any longer along the sea front. However, Fraser had other plans. There was no question but that Spider was a big draw and he could prove to be equally popular at night-time in the pubs and clubs around the town amongst those people who were in the frame of mind to enjoy themselves. As for Spider, he was beside himself with frustration. There had not been one single opportunity for escape. The photographer seemed to have guessed his intentions and, if anything, guarded against the eventuality with extra vigilance. The truth was that the monkey had proved to be a clever investment and Fraser was going to capitalize on it for all its worth. There was no way he was going to slip up. Spider was well looked after; yet the unfortunate animal was bored out of his mind.

*

During all these weeks Pebble had continued his laborious progress across country. The evenings were less warm than before and he had begun to feel a little torpid. But then as soon as the sun shone on him again, he (as far as he was able) livened up. By October the windmill loomed huge and black directly ahead of him. Poor Pebble wasn't to know what a bitter disappointment lay in store there. The thought of meeting his old friends once again was what cheered him on more than anything.

'They must have been waiting an age for me,' the tortoise said to himself. 'They're so much speedier than me, all of them. Still, I'm nearly there. Good old friends, how glad I shall be to see them!'

He put on a final spurt, tortoise-style, and in another week he was up against the walls of the fabled windmill. He blinked about him. He saw no pets. He was very, very tired and evening was coming on.

'I know they must be just around the corner,' Pebble told himself, 'but I really don't think I can manage another step today. I'll have a snooze now and search them out tomorrow.' He withdrew into his shell right there and then, pleased that his epic trek was ended. 'And if they should find me in the meantime,' he murmured in a muffled voice, 'well, they can very soon wake me.'

It was a chill night and Pebble went into a deep sleep. The sun was well up before he struggled back to consciousness. He was feeling very sluggish. 'My word,' he muttered, 'that was some sleep! Now I mustn't lose any more time. I'll find something to nibble and I expect I'll bump into them while I'm doing it.' He made a circumference of the windmill, pecking now and then at a weed, and arrived back where he'd started without a glimpse of company.

'Strange,' he mused.'Those pens are a bit like what we were used to in the pet shop. But there's nothing in any of them. I'm not sure what to do. Perhaps I'd better just sit tight and wait. I won't go wandering off in case we miss each other.'

He waited and waited and no one showed up. He was still waiting at dusk. He felt peculiarly languid. 'Surely,' he yawned, 'I can't be the *first* one here?'

That night there was a real nip of autumn in the air and Pebble, out in the open with nothing to cover him, suffered acute discomfort. The next day his instinct drove him to find some sort of protective nest. His movements had become even slower than usual.

'What is this windmill thing anyway?' he asked himself. 'There's no sign of life here at all. Oh dear, I hope the others didn't give up on me.' He crawled into some dry dead vegetation only a metre or two away and nestled into it. He felt as if he really didn't want to stir from it again. 'They'll have to . . . come looking . . . if they want to . . . find me,' he said. 'I can't ever . . . catch them up.' His body seemed to go all numb and the next instant he fell into a dreamless sleep, deeper and deeper and deeper. . . .

One evening Spider found himself with the photographer in the bar of The Derby Arms. It was a pub Fraser frequented and he took along his camera and other equipment in the hope that some of the other regulars would be tempted to have their pictures taken with the monkey in favourite convivial surroundings. He was not disappointed. Spider was made to pose with the eager customers, sometimes singly and sometimes in a group, as well as with the landlord and his wife.

'This is the way to make money,' Fraser joked. 'I've never had a better excuse for going to the pub!'

Later, he and Margot calculated how many other similar sources there were to be tapped in the vicinity. They drew up quite a list.

Fraser chuckled. 'You know what's just occurred to me?' he said.

'No, what?' Margot smiled.

'Why don't I pay that brother of yours a visit at the Darts Club? Then he can see just how professional the monkey's become. I won't forewarn him. I'll just turn up out of the blue. He'll kick himself for only taking fifty quid off me when he finds out how well we've been doing.' Fraser chortled.

'So *that's* what you paid for him,' Margot said slyly. 'You let that slip out, didn't you?'

Fraser shrugged. 'Peanuts,' he said. 'Margot, we're coining it.'

The Darts Club met on a Tuesday at The Tudor Close, an old inn near the school where Gilson was caretaker. Fraser and Spider arrived mid-evening, just when the members were in their highest spirits. Spider still loathed the car and had been jittery all the way during the drive. Fraser was aware of it and shortened Spider's chain as a precaution, wrapping most of it round his fist.

The atmosphere in the inn was lively but the air

was stale and sour with the smell of beer. There was a fog of tobacco smoke, yet only one small window had been opened overlooking the beer garden. Spider was very much on edge. He sensed something threatening. Gilson wasn't playing darts when Fraser walked in, but he didn't notice the photographer at first because he was watching the match that was in progress. Fraser bought himself a drink and a bag of peanuts for Spider. The monkey wasn't interested in them. He was far too tense. Suddenly Gilson swung round and came towards the bar. Spider saw him and began visibly to quake. He had never forgotten the look of the man who had ill-treated him.

'Hello, John,' Fraser called. 'Come and renew your acquaintance with my assistant.'

'Bob!' Gilson cried. 'I didn't know you were here. When did you arrive?'

'Just a minute ago.'

Gilson peered at the monkey. 'Why didn't you let me know?'

'I wanted to surprise you. What do you think of him?'

'What do *you* think of him's more to the point, isn't it?' Gilson returned.

'John, he's the best investment I ever made,' Fraser said, savouring every word. 'I'll clean up with this one.'

'Yeh?' Gilson didn't look too happy. 'Well, I thought you might. Does he still bite?' He was staring right at Spider who was baring his teeth.

'Certainly not. He loves people,' Fraser enthused. 'You should see him playing up to them. He's a born model, too.'

Gilson stretched out a hand. Spider shifted his position on Fraser's shoulder, looking round for somewhere to jump. Gilson wanted to pat him but Spider suspected a blow. He opened his mouth and gave the man a nasty nip on one finger. Gilson howled and Spider leapt down, yanking the chain hard. Fraser had shortened the chain so much the monkey couldn't reach the ground and he dangled in mid-air, choking; the collar tightened round his throat.

'Let him go, you're strangling him!' a woman shrieked.

Fraser unwound the chain in haste and the second Spider felt his feet touch the ground he bounded away with such speed that the chain was pulled right out of Fraser's grip.

'Catch him, someone!' the photographer yelled.

But Spider had seen the open window and, trailing the chain, he was up on the sill and through the window in a trice, before anyone had time to look round.

'You damn fool, John!' Fraser swore. 'What the hell did you want to meddle for?' He was furious. He dashed out of the pub and round to the garden. In the darkness Spider was difficult to see, but Fraser could hear him all right. The trailing chain rattled along the ground to mark the monkey's escape route. However, he was far too quick for the photographer. In no time he had put the pub and all its occupants well behind him and was once more in open country.

Spider's first priority was to make sure he wasn't being followed. The sight of the caretaker had been like a nightmare to him, and now he ran and ran until

158

the frightening vision had faded somewhat from his mind. The horrible chain chinked and clanked behind him but, until his initial shock was subsided, the monkey was quite oblivious of it.

He came past the school where he had played with the children. He remembered everything that had happened there and raced on past. Now he began to tire, finding the trailing chain irksome. He stopped in the darkness and pulled the thing towards him. He bit at it and pulled at it, but it was beyond his ability or strength to loosen it. Spider screamed in vexation. How could he rid himself of it?

He knew he was back in the area where he and the other pets had sampled the taste of freedom. It all seemed so long ago. Where were they? What had happened to them? Spider knew there was one way of finding out. Moving more slowly now he continued on his way, once again in the direction of the windmill. His body cooled down and, for the first time, he became aware of the cold. He didn't dare to stop again. He had to get there. Only there could he hope for release from the chain and for the sort of comfort and shelter and affection he had once known, far back in his memory.

18

Rescue

The Windmill Pet Shop couldn't quite settle back into its old routine. For a start, two of its occupants were still missing. And then, there was the question of the name. Eric's thoughts on that had been communicated to the shop's owner.

'I suppose you're right,' Dobson conceded. 'We are only a supply shop now.'

'Shall we change it then?'

Dobson sighed. 'I don't know,' he said. 'Is it worth it?' He left the day-to-day running of the shop almost entirely to Eric now.

'Of course it's worth it,' Eric replied at once. 'We can build the business up, Mr Dobson. We're still the only pet shop—' he paused to smile ruefully, 'in Wandle. People depend on us.'

Dobson nodded slowly, one finger tickling Auntie's pate as she perched by the till.

'WINDMILL PET SHOP,' Auntie mused. The two men laughed.

'*She'd* never get used to the change, anyway,' Dobson remarked, jokily. He was lighter in spirit these days for, despite the sadness of Spider's disappearance, the recovery of Auntie and the smaller animals was a great joy to him. Besides, he hadn't entirely given up on the monkey. And there was something else. Something of Eric's enthusiasm had transmitted itself to him. It was too late for the old man to begin anew but Eric had youth on his side.

'We could make other changes too,' Eric said daringly. He had plans. He held his breath.

'Other changes?' Dobson pulled at his moustache. 'What changes?'

'Well, you see,' Eric said slowly to avoid betraying his tenseness, 'we're rather old-fashioned.' He had begun to use the words 'we' and 'us' quite a lot lately. 'The layout, I mean. Oh, all sorts of things.'

'Yes, yes, I know.' Dobson nodded. 'It's me, Eric. *I'm* old-fashioned.'

Eric grinned. 'I'm not,' he declared.

Dobson looked at him, long and hard. But he didn't argue. And that was how things stood.

The cold had taken Spider by surprise. The clear skies late on in the year meant the temperature plummeted at night. Spider had never been exposed to such conditions before. He kept going, thinking only of the relief he would find at his destination. One thing bothered him apart from the cold. He remembered Auntie's description of the windmill as being quite empty. He couldn't really believe that she had understood what she was looking for, since he hadn't been there to guide her. But the notion nagged at him and urged him on to his own discovery.

The first faint streaks of dawn found Spider running through the overgrown orchard near the

161

windmill. He recognized it, despite its altered appearance, since he had been there last, nine months before. He approached the windmill itself hesitantly, almost afraid to confirm what his senses were telling him. He noticed the abandoned hutches. Everything about the place suggested neglect and lifelessness. Spider pressed himself against a door, shivering miserably in the growing light. There was nothing to break the all-pervading silence, not even the early chirping of a bird. Spider sat immobile on the doorstep of the now unoccupied building that had once been his home. There he and his old master – the kindly, solitary custodian of an animal sanctuary for unwanted or injured creatures – had lived happily. Spider's one great purpose of returning himself to his old life, his old home, had come to nothing.

He had wanted the other animals to share this home with him. Only he knew how much more secure, how much more comfortable they would have been. He had wanted to see them arrive, one by one, having earned the hospitality he was offering them. Then they could have looked back together over the countryside they had crossed to the pet shop where it had all begun – where the foolish dream had been born that would now never be fulfilled. And where were the animals? Where was Auntie? Had they come here, struggling across that landscape, only to find a disappointment, a sort of bleakness at the end of it? If they had, they had very soon left again. Spider pictured them wandering aimlessly through the countryside with all sense of direction lost.

The sun rose higher, spreading its warmth over the sad huddled figure with the long trailing chain. It was a very warm day. At last Spider stirred himself. He seemed to become suddenly aware of his predicament as he stared at the hateful chain. Now there was no one to release him from it and, worse, no one to take him in from the cold that he knew must return. He decided to have a look round, just in case there was any trace remaining to tell him that the animals had been there. He crept round the windmill. Nothing. Then he started to look farther afield, calling them by name as he did so. He thought there was the slightest chance they might be in hiding. There was no answer.

'It's no use,' he said to himself. 'I'm alone.' But then he detected a hint of movement amongst some vegetation.

Pebble, warmed by the sun and only semi-dormant, heard Spider's calls. They pierced his consciousness as if from a very great distance, but they were enough to interrupt his sleep. The next moment Spider was there, pulling off the vegetation with haste to reveal the tortoise who, the monkey thought, looked more dead than alive.

'Pebble!' he cried. 'You're here! But only you?'

The tortoise wasn't yet sufficiently awake to recognize what was happening.

'Oh, you're dying, you're dying,' Spider wailed. 'It's all my fault!' He knew nothing about hibernation. 'But perhaps it's not too late. Perhaps I can save you! Yes, yes, I must save you!' He picked up the comatose reptile and cradled him in his arms. Pebble's eyes opened. His legs waved feebly.

'There's life in you yet,' Spider said gleefully. 'And

163

now I have a new purpose. The cold won't kill Pebble while Spider's still around!'

Without a backward glance at the desolate windmill he began to descend the hillock, the chain always bumping along behind him. In his new mood of selflessness it didn't even occur to Spider that the haven he knew existed for Pebble could also free him from his own horrible shackles. Presently the tortoise came to himself and was startled to see a kindly, well-remembered face so close to his own.

'Spider!' he gasped. 'But how. . . ? Where did. . . ?'

'Hush, Pebble. You just rest where you are. I'll tell you everything in time. But first, where are the others?'

'I don't know. There was no one at the windmill. It took me an age to get there, Spider. I think they gave up on me. But – I don't understand. There's nothing there. Why did we all have to go there?'

'All in good time,' said Spider. 'There is an explanation. Let me first tell you my adventures. And then we'll think about our friends. There's plenty of time for everything on the way back to the pet shop.'

Other great reads *from* **Red Fox**

Further Red Fox titles that you might enjoy reading are listed on the following pages. They are available in bookshops or they can be ordered directly from us.

   If you would like to order books, please send this form and the money due to:

ARROW BOOKS, BOOKSERVICE BY POST, PO BOX 29, DOUGLAS, ISLE OF MAN, BRITISH ISLES. Please enclose a cheque or postal order made out to Arrow Books Ltd for the amount due, plus 30p per book for postage and packing to a maximum of £3.00, both for orders within the UK. For customers outside the UK, please allow 35p per book.

NAME _____

ADDRESS _____

_____

Please print clearly.

Whilst every effort is made to keep prices low, it is sometimes necessary to increase cover prices at short notice. If you are ordering books by post, to save delay it is advisable to phone to confirm the correct price. The number to ring is THE SALES DEPARTMENT 071 (if outside London) 973 9700.

Other great reads **from Red Fox**

Discover the great animal stories of Colin Dann

JUST NUFFIN

The Summer holidays loomed ahead with nothing to look forward to except one dreary week in a caravan with only Mum and Dad for company. Roger was sure he'd be bored.

But then Dad finds Nuffin: an abandoned puppy who's more a bundle of skin and bones than a dog. Roger's holiday is transformed and he and Nuffin are inseparable. But Dad is adamant that Nuffin must find a new home. Is there *any* way Roger can persuade him to change his mind?

ISBN 0 09 966900 5   £2.99

KING OF THE VAGABONDS

'You're very young,' Sammy's mother said, 'so heed my advice. Don't go into Quartermile Field.'

His mother and sister are happily domesticated but Sammy, the tabby cat, feels different. They are content with their lot, never wondering what lies beyond their immediate surroundings. But Sammy is burningly curious and his life seems full of mysteries. Who is his father? Where has he gone? And what is the mystery of Quartermile Field?

ISBN 0 09 957190 0   £2.99

Other great reads ✦ *from* **Red Fox**

Fantasy fiction—the Song of the Lioness series

ALANNA—THE FIRST ADVENTURE
Tamora Pierce

Alanna has just one wish—to become a knight. Her twin brother, Thom, prefers magic and wants to be a great sorcerer. So they swop places and Alanna, dressed as a boy, sets off for the king's court. Becoming a knight is difficult—but Alanna is brave and determined to succeed. And her gift for magic is to prove essential to her survival . . .

ISBN 0 09 943560 8   £2.50

IN THE HAND OF THE GODDESS
Tamora Pierce

Alan of Trebond is the smallest but toughest of the squires at court. Only Prince Jonathan knows she is really a girl called Alanna.

As she prepares for her final training to become a knight, Alanna is troubled. Is she the only one to sense the evil in Duke Roger? Does no one realise what a threat his steely ambition poses?

Alanna must use every ounce of her warrior skills and her gift for magic if she is to survive her Ordeal of Knighthood—and outwit the dangerous sorcerer duke.

ISBN 0 09 955560 3   £2.50

The third and fourth titles in the Song of the Lioness series, **THE GIRL WHO RODE LIKE A MAN** and **LIONESS RAMPANT** will be published by Red Fox in July 1992.

Other great reads from **Red Fox**

THE SNIFF STORIES   Ian Whybrow

Things just keep happening to Ben Moore. It's dead hard avoiding disaster when you've got to keep your street cred with your mates *and* cope with a family of oddballs at the same time. There's his appalling 2½ year old sister, his scatty parents who are into healthy eating and animal rights and, worse than all of these, there's Sniff! If only Ben could just get on with his scientific experiments and his attempt at a world beating *Swampbeast* score . . . but there's no chance of that while chaos is just around the corner.

ISBN 0 09 975040 6   £2.99

J.B. SUPERSLEUTH   Joan Davenport

James Bond is a small thirteen-year-old with spots and spectacles. But with a name like that, how can he help being a supersleuth?

It all started when James and 'Polly' (Paul) Perkins spotted a teacher's stolen car. After that, more and more mysteries needed solving. With the case of the Arabian prince, the Murdered Model, the Bonfire Night Murder and the Lost Umbrella, JB's reputation at Moorside Comprehensive soars.

But some of the cases aren't quite what they seem . . .

ISBN 0 09 971780 8   £2.99

Other great reads from **Red Fox**

THE WINTER VISITOR   Joan Lingard

Strangers didn't come to Nick Murray's home town in winter.
And they didn't lodge at his house. But Ed Black had—and Nick
Murray didn't like it.

Why had Ed come? The small Scottish seaside resort was
bleak, cold and grey at that time of year. The answer, Nick
begins to suspect, lies with his mother—was there some past
connection between her and Ed?

ISBN 0 09 938590 2   £1.99

STRANGERS IN THE HOUSE   Joan Lingard

Calum resents his mother remarrying. He doesn't want to move
to a flat in Edinburgh with a new father and a thirteen-year-old
stepsister. Stella, too, dreads the new marriage. Used to living
alone with her father she loathes the idea of sharing their small
flat.

Stella's and Calum's struggles to adapt to a new life, while
trying to cope with the problems of growing up are related with
great poignancy in a book which will be enjoyed by all older
readers.

ISBN 0 09 955020 2   £2.99

Other great reads from **Red Fox**

School stories from Enid Blyton

THE NAUGHTIEST GIRL IN THE SCHOOL

'Mummy, if you send me away to school, I shall be so naughty
there, they'll have to send me back home again,' said Elizabeth.
And when her parents won't be budged, Elizabeth sets out to
do just that—she stirs up trouble all around her and gets the
name of the bold bad schoolgirl. She's sure she's longing to
go home—but to her surprise there are some things she hadn't
reckoned with. Like making friends . . .

ISBN 0 09 945500 5   £2.99

THE NAUGHTIEST GIRL IS A MONITOR

'Oh dear, I wish I wasn't a monitor! I wish I could go to a
monitor for help! I can't even think what I ought to do!'

When Elizabeth Allen is chosen to be a monitor in her third
term at Whyteleafe School, she tries to do her best. But
somehow things go wrong and soon she is in just as much trouble
as she was in her first term, when she was the naughtiest girl
in the school!

ISBN 0 09 945490 4   £2.99